Happy Birthday, Mallory!

by Laurie Friedman

illustrations by Tamara Schmitz

darbycreek

MINNEAPOLIS

CONTENTS

A WORD FROM MALLORY

Some people might say eight is great, but for me, eight was a really, really, really hard year. Just about everything in my life changed.

First, I had to move to a new town and leave behind my best friend, Mary Ann. Then had to go to a new school. And to top things off, my big brother, Max, got a dog even though we already had a cat . . . my cat, Cheeseburger. But now I'm turning nine, and I know nine will be just fine because I'm planning to make nine the best year ever.

And to kick it off, I'm planning the best-ever celebration.

It all started tonight when Grandma called.

"I can't believe that in one month, my little Honey Bee will be nine years old. That's so exciting...I bet you can hardly wait!"

And when Grandma said the part about me being hardly able to wait, I started thinking . . . maybe I shouldn't wait. Maybe I should start celebrating right away.

The more I thought about it, the more I liked the idea. So I made a decision: Starting tomorrow, I'm going to start celebrating.

For my ninth birthday, I'm not going to just celebrate my birth day. I'm going to celebrate my birth month!

And that's when I realized, I'd better get busy. A birth month celebration takes a lot of planning. But I have a feeling if I plan it all out, it will be the world's best, best, best birth month ever.

Because if you plan it all out, nothing can go wrong.

Right?

A PERFECT PLAN

"Mom, Dad, wake up!" I bounce on my parents' bed until they start to move. "Do you know what day it is today?"

Mom opens her eyes, but she looks confused. "Monday?"

"It's Monday," I say. "But do you know why this Monday is different than all other Mondays?"

Dad rolls over and looks at the clock on his nightstand. "Mallory, on all other Mondays, we wake up at seven o'clock. It's 6:15 in the morning! What is so important about this Monday that you needed to wake us up so early?"

I plop down on the bed between Mom and Dad. "Today is the first day of my birth month celebration!"

I wait for my parents to say, *"Wow, the first day of your birth month celebration. That is so,*

so, so exciting!" But that's not what they say.

"What's a birth month celebration?" mumbles Dad.

"It's when you celebrate the *month* you were born, not just the *day*," I tell him.

Dad rolls his pillow into a ball and puts his head back on it. "Mallory, a *day* celebration is plenty."

"But I want my ninth year to be the best ever, so I'm planning to start it off with the best-ever celebration." I pull a sheet of paper out of one of my slippers and unfold it. "And I think I've come up with a perfect plan."

Mom sits up in bed and turns on a light. Dad sits up too. They look at each other, and then they look at me. "What did you have in mind?" Dad asks me.

I snuggle up between my parents and tell them exactly what I have in mind.

10 Ways I, Mallory McDonald, Plan to Celebrate My 9th Birth Month.

Way #1: By eating ALL the junk food I want.

Way #2: By watching TV for as long as I'd like.

Way #3: By staying home from school on Fridays.

Way #4: By painting my room light purple. (Dad can help.)

Way #5: By not doing my chores. (Max can help.)

Way #6: By getting my ears pierced. (V.I.W.) Very Important Way!

Way #7: By celebrating with a gift-of-the-day.

Way #8: By having a surprise party.

Way #9: By Mary Ann coming to visit on my birthday.

Way #10: By celebrating with a cake-of-the-week.

When I finish reading my list, my parents look at each other like they just came out of a parent-teacher conference, and there's something they need to talk to me about.

"Mallory," says Mom. "I know you're excited about turning nine. But we need to go through your list and talk about what's reasonable and what's unreasonable."

"I already went through my list," I tell Mom. "I crossed off the unreasonable stuff, like putting a hot fudge fountain in the backyard."

Mom reaches for my list. "I think we better do this together."

Mom looks at my list. "Mallory, you can't eat all the junk food you want. You can't watch all the TV you'd like. And unless you have a fever, you know you have to go to school *every* day."

I start to explain that all of these things are important because they are part of my birth month celebration, but Mom doesn't let me. She looks at my list again, and says my name slowly like she's talking to a two-year-old and not an almost nine-year-old.

"MAL-LOR-Y! We just painted your room. We're not going to repaint it. And your brother does not have to do all your chores for a month. How would you feel if you had to do all of Max's chores for a month?"

I wouldn't want to do that. I don't really want Max to have to do mine, but I don't think Mom understands that a celebration isn't a celebration unless you do something to celebrate it. I point to Way #7 on my list. "Can I get my ears pierced?"

Mom rubs the sides of her head, like she has a headache that won't go away.

"Mallory, we've talked about this. You can't get your ears pierced until you're twelve."

"But Mom! Getting my ears pierced is one of the most important ways I want to celebrate my birth month."

Mom shakes her head. "No pierced ears!" She hands the list to Dad.

He starts reading. "A gift of-the-day sounds like a nice idea." Dad rumples my hair. "How about a hug and a kiss . . . every day?"

"Not that kind of gift," I tell Dad.

"Sweet Potato," says Dad, "I've never heard of a month-long celebration that includes a gift a day."

"Let's talk about your party," says Mom.

"I know you've already planned my skating party," I say. "But what I really want is a surprise party."

"Mallory, you can't plan your own surprise party. If you do, you won't be surprised."

"I'll act surprised," I tell Mom. "Watch."

I stand up on the bed between Mom and Dad and put my hands on my cheeks. "I can't believe it!" I suck in air while I'm talking so I don't just look surprised. I sound surprised too. "All this for *me?*"

I look around the bedroom like I'm looking at friends and presents and decorations that I didn't expect to see. "I am just so, so, so surprised!"

Dad laughs. "Mallory, you are very good at acting surprised, but we've already planned your skating party."

"Turning nine is a big deal," I explain to Dad. "I want *everything* to be perfect."

"*Everything* will be great. We had a skating party for Max when he turned nine,

and it was a lot of fun."

I look down and pick a fuzz ball off the blanket. "I want this year to be better than last year, so it's important that it starts with the best-ever celebration. I've told you lots of ways I want to celebrate and you've said *no* to everything."

Mom looks at the list again. "Having Mary Ann visit is a nice idea. I'll call her mom and see if they can come down for your birthday weekend."

"I hope she can come." I look down and pick another fuzz ball off the blanket. "I can't imagine my birthday without my best friend."

"I'll call today," says Mom.

Dad clears his throat like he's a judge and he's about to say something important to the people in his courtroom. "Mallory, celebrations are nice. But whatever you do to celebrate your birthday won't affect the way your year turns out."

I know you're not supposed to argue with a judge, but I think Dad is wrong.

"Dad, it's like studying for a test," I say. "If you study, you make a good grade. If you plan a good celebration, you have a good year."

Dad pats me on the head, like he heard what I said but he doesn't agree. "I think we've had enough birthday talk for one morning. Why don't you go get dressed?"

I start to go downstairs. Then I stop.

"Wait a minute," I say. "What about Way #10? Celebrating each week of my birth month with a cake-of-the-week?"

Mom laughs. "A cake a week sounds like a sweet idea."

I can't believe Mom said *yes* to something. "Can we have a cake on Saturday?"

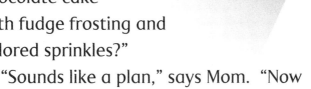

"I don't see why not," says Mom.

Now it's my turn to smile. "Can we have chocolate cake with fudge frosting and colored sprinkles?"

"Sounds like a plan," says Mom. "Now go get ready for school."

"OK," I tell Mom. But as I walk down the stairs, there's only one thing I can think about getting ready for, and that's my birth month celebration.

I've got a lot to do if it's going to be the best, best, best celebration ever.

MALLORY ON A MISSION

I'm on a mission. A *make-sure-everybody-knows-it's-my-birth-month* mission. There are a lot of people who I want to be part of my celebration. I split my mission into five parts.

MALLORY'S MISSION: PART I
   Target: My brother, Max
   Location: Our bathroom sink

When I walk into the bathroom, Max is already brushing his teeth. His dog, Champ, is with him.

I squirt toothpaste onto my toothbrush. "Guess what?" I say to Max. "I'm celebrating my birth month this year, not just my birth day. And today is the official start of my celebration."

Max spits into the sink. "Guess what? I'm skipping school and going fishing."

Sometimes Max says such dumb things.

"You can't skip school and go fishing."

"Well, you can't celebrate your birthday for a month." Max wipes off his mouth with the back of his hand.

"Give me three good reasons why not!"

Max rolls his eyes. "Because it's dumb. Because it's stupid. And because Mom and Dad won't let you."

I finish brushing and stick my toothbrush into my hole in the toothbrush holder.

"Mom already said I can have a cake a week during my birth month. I'm having my first cake on Saturday, and since you're my only brother, I want to make sure you'll be there to wish me *Happy Birth Month*."

I reach down and pet Champ. "He's invited too."

"Did you say you're having a cake a week for your birth month?"

I nod.

"And Mom agreed to that?"

I nod again. "Max, I'm turning nine. This is a very important celebration."

Max rolls his eyes. "I'm turning eleven, and you don't see me celebrating my birthday for a month. And the last time I checked, nine was no big deal."

Max might not think nine is a big deal now, but he will on Saturday when he has a big piece of chocolate cake on his plate.

Part I of my mission is complete. On to Part II.

MALLORY'S MISSION: PART II

Target: My next-door neighbors, Joey and
Winnie Winston

Location: On our way to school

"Knock, knock," I say as we walk toward Fern Falls Elementary.

"Who's there?" asks Joey.

"Itzmy," I say smiling.

"Itzmy?" Winnie repeats the name like it's the title of a boring book she has to read for school and not the first part of a

knock-knock joke.

Joey ignores his sister. "Itzmy who?" he asks.

"It's my birth month celebration starting today," I tell them. "I'm having a cake a week. My first one is on Saturday, and you're both invited."

Winnie's lip curls up like a sleeping bag. "Who ever heard of celebrating a birth month? Count me out. I've got more important things to do, like brush my hair." Winnie walks ahead of Joey and me.

I look at Joey. "Can you come on Saturday?"

"I don't know," he says. "I'm supposed to go ice skating with Pete on Saturday."

"C'mon! I'll make sure you get an extra-big piece."

Joey's been a great friend ever since I moved to Fern Falls. I know he'll be there.

Part II of my mission is complete. Now, it's time for Part III.

MALLORY'S MISSION: PART III

Target: My desk mate, Pamela

Location: Fern Falls Elementary, Room 310

As soon as I walk into my classroom, Mrs. Daily tells us to open our science books to page ninety-six. "Today, we're starting our unit on astronauts and space," she says.

I open up my science book and turn the pages slowly. It's not that I mind learning about astronauts and space, but what I really want to do is invite Pamela to my birth month celebration.

I just don't want to celebrate without her.

Mrs. Daily starts reading about rockets. I start a note to my desk mate.

Pamela,

I am celebrating my birth month, which starts TODAY!!!!!!

Can you come to a celebration at my house on Saturday?

Hugs, Mallory

I fold my note into a tiny square and pass it to Pamela. When she's done reading, she turns it over and writes something on the back, then refolds the piece of paper and passes it back to me.

Mallory,

Happy birth month!

I would love to help you celebrate, but I have a violin lesson on Saturday.

I have to talk to my mom.

Hugs back, Pamela

When I finish reading, I smile at Pamela. *"See you Saturday,"* I mouth to her.

I know Pamela's mom will let her come to my house. Everyone knows a birth month celebration is a lot more important than a violin lesson.

Part III of my mission is complete. On to Part IV.

MALLORY'S MISSION: PART IV

Target: Grandma

Location: On the phone

When I get home from school, I don't even stop for a snack. I go straight to the phone and dial Grandma's number.

When she answers, I tell her right away about the special celebration I have planned. "Grandma, I decided to celebrate my birth month this year!"

And before Grandma has a chance to say anything, my birth month plans start spilling out of my mouth like chocolate chips falling from an open bag. "I'm having a cake a week, and Mary Ann might come to visit, and I'm having a party!" I tell her.

"Slow down," says Grandma.

But once I get started, it's hard to slow down. "Even though I really wanted to have a surprise party, I'm having a skating party. And I know you live a long way away, but I wanted to know if you can come to my party."

Grandma sighs into the phone. "Honey Bee, I do live a long way away, but I'm planning to send you something special for your birthday this year."

I smile into the phone. "Can you give me a hint about what you're sending?"

Grandma laughs. "No hints. But I think you'll like it."

Knowing Grandma, I'm sure I will. I tell Grandma good-bye, then I head to my room. There's still one very important person that needs to know about my birth month celebration.

MALLORY'S MISSION: PART V
Target: My best, best, best friend, Mary Ann
Location: My desk in my room

Dear Mary Ann,

I have something important to tell you. I'm celebrating my birth month this year!

I know that's not something we've done before, but I decided to do things differently this year.

If you're wondering why, I'll tell you.

Being eight was my worst, worst, worst year ever!!! If I had to rate it, I'd give it a big thumbs-down. (moving and leaving you was the worst part!)

I want to make nine the best year ever, so I'm planning to start it off with the best-ever celebration!

Even though mom said no to lots of ways that I want to celebrate, like getting my ears pierced (she said I have to wait until I'm twelve) and having a surprise party (she already planned a skating party), she said yes to you coming to visit on my birthday!

I hope your mom says you can come!

WRITE ME AS SOON AS YOU KNOW IF YOU ARE COMING!

Biggest, hugest hugs and kisses ever,
mallory

P.S. Here's something mom said yes to: a cake-a-week for my birth month! This Saturday I'm having my first cake, chocolate with sprinkles! It will be great except for one thing: NO YOU! BOO-HOO!

I finish my letter and stick it in an envelope. Max, Joey, Winnie, Pamela,

Grandma, and Mary Ann all know about my special celebration. Now I feel like my birth month can begin. I put my hands behind my head and my feet on my desk, like I've seen detectives do on TV when they crack a case.

"Cheeseburger," I say to my cat, "mission accomplished."

SADDER DAY

"AH-CHOO!"

That makes sixty-seven times Mom has sneezed since she woke up this morning. I walk into the den with a box of tissues.

"AH-CHOO!"

Sixty-eight.

I hand Mom the box.

Mom looks at me. At least she tries to look at me, but her eyes are all puffy and swollen from coughing and sneezing.

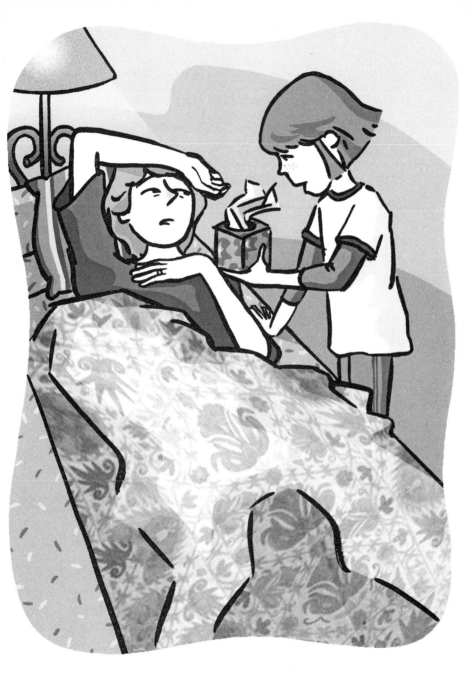

"Mallory, I know you're disappointed. I'm sorry today isn't going like you wanted it to."

Mom is right. Today *isn't* going like I wanted it to. Today is Saturday, but it should be called "*Sadder Day*." Today is a whole lot sadder than I thought it would be.

Today is the day I was supposed to be enjoying a cake-of-the-week with my friends and family. Right now, my mouth should be filled with the taste of chocolate cake and fudge frosting. But right now, my mouth is empty.

"Don't look so glum," says Dad. He walks into the den and hands me an envelope with my name on it. "The postman paid you a visit."

I take my envelope, walk into the kitchen, and sit down at the table.

I didn't get a cake-of-the-week, but at least I get a letter from my best friend.

Dear Mallory,

Happy, happy, happy birth month!!!!!!

Are you having the best birth month ever? I bet you are.

I have some very happy birth month news that I know you will like hearing.

I'M COMING TO VISIT! Did your mom tell you yet? My mom said we can come for your whole birth weekend! (I figured there must be such a thing as a birth weekend since there is such a thing as a birth month.)

I wanted to come for the whole month. Mom said no to that, but she did say I will be there for your skating party! I am so, so, so excited! I don't think it matters that you're not having a surprise party. Skating parties are fun, too!

See you soon, soon, soon!

Hugs and kisses,

Mary Ann

P.S. How was your cake-of-the-week?
I want to hear about it, down to the very last
sprinkle.

P.P.S. I hope you took
pictures when you blew
out your candles. When
I come visit, we can
make a birth month
scrapbook.

P.P.P.S. Tell your mom that nine is OLD
to get your ears pierced. I got mine pierced
when I was eight. Remember? Maybe you
should try asking your mom in a different way.
I just know she'll say yes!

I reread the letter from Mary Ann. Then
I take a sheet of paper from Mom's desk
and start writing.

Dear Mary Ann,

I have some bad, bad, bad news.

My birth month isn't going like I had planned.

It's a long, sad story. But since you're my best friend, I'll tell it to you anyway.

I didn't get a cake-of-the-week because Mom didn't bake a cake-of-the-week because she has the flu.

Even if she had baked it, no one would have come to eat it, because Joey had other plans and Pamela had violin lessons and Max and Winnie both said it was dumb.

Since I didn't have a cake, I don't have any pictures to put in my birth month scrapbook.

I hope this story did not make you too sad. I am counting the days and minutes and seconds until you get here.

Mallory

P.S. mom hasn't said yes to getting my ears pierced yet, but I think she will. (See plan below for how I'm going to ask her.)

Operation Earrings

I finish my letter to Mary Ann, fold it, and stick it in the envelope.

The first week of my birth month wasn't so great. I try not to think about what *didn't* happen and instead think about all the good things that are *going* to happen.

I think about the cake-of-the-week I'm going to have next week. I think about the class party I'm going to have the week after that. I think about Mary Ann coming to visit. Then, I think about how much fun it will be to have pierced ears.

I reach up and feel the soft, floppy part of my earlobes.

Tonight . . . I will put Operation Earrings into action.

Tomorrow . . . there will be holes where today there were none.

THE HOLE STORY

"Good morning, class," says Mrs. Daily. "How was everyone's weekend?"

Room 310 fills up with *goods* and *greats* and *supers* and *terrifics*. There are even a few *amazings*. But I'm quiet. I wouldn't describe the first weekend of my birth month as good or great or super or terrific, and definitely not amazing.

"What did everyone do?" asks Mrs. Daily.

"I went ice skating," says Joey.

"Me too," says Pete.

"I took a violin lesson," calls out Pamela.

"We went shopping," says Danielle.

"Shoe shopping," says Arielle.

Both girls stick their feet in the air to show the class their matching sneakers.

Mrs. Daily smiles at Danielle and Arielle's feet.

Then she smiles at me. "Mallory, what did you do this weekend?"

All I can think about is what I *didn't* do. "Nothing," I mumble.

"Well, I'm sure you did something," says Mrs. Daily. She picks up a piece of chalk and writes *What I Did This Weekend* on the chalkboard.

"Class, this morning, I'd like you all to write a one-page essay on what you did

this weekend. Use details about what happened to make the reader feel like they were there with you."

Everyone takes out paper and pencils, but not me. I don't get out anything to write with because I don't have anything to write about. Mrs. Daily comes over to my desk. "Having trouble getting started?"

I nod.

"Think for a minute," says Mrs. Daily.
"You'll come up with something."

"I know what Mallory can write about,"
says Pamela. "She's turning nine soon.
She can write about what she did this
weekend to celebrate her birthday."

Pamela winks at me like she knows
what I did this weekend. But what Pamela
doesn't know is that I didn't do anything.

Mrs. Daily clears her throat. "Mallory, what do you think of that idea?"

I think about my weekend. I didn't get a cake. I tried to talk to Mom about getting my ears pierced. But that didn't work either.

"Mrs. Daily, would it be OK if I write about what I *didn't* do this weekend?"

Mrs. Daily says if that's what I remember

about my weekend, then I can certainly write about it. I take out a sheet of paper and begin.

The Hole Story
By Mallory McDonald
Author's Note: You will need tissues when you read this story. It is very sad!

Once upon a time, there was a little girl who was about to turn nine. All she wanted for her birthday were two little holes, one in each ear. So one weekend, she asked her mother if she could get these two little holes.

Her mother said, "NO! You may not have two little holes, one in each ear, until you turn twelve."

So the little girl did what any other

little girl who was about to turn nine (and wanted something really, really, really badly) would do.

She begged and pleaded with her mother.

Her mother still said, "NO!"

So then, the little girl scrubbed the floor. That was how she spent her weekend. SCRUBBING THE FLOOR! She hoped this would get her mother to change her mind.

But guess what? It didn't work. Her mother still said, "NO!" (This was mean and cruel of her mother, don't you think?)

So the little girl offered to pay for the holes in her ears with her very own allowance money and eat spinach if her mother would just let her get those two tiny, little holes. But her mother still said, "NO!"

The little girl was starting to think things were hopeless. But she didn't give up.

She told her mother that the only thing she would need to make her birth month (which hadn't been so great so far) extra-special would be those two little holes.

You won't believe what happened next.

You will never EVER guess.

Her mother still said, "NO!" And, to top it off, she sent the girl to her room for not listening the first time.

When that happened, a tear ran down the girl's cheek. She had no choice but to wipe it away and move on with her life.

The moral of the story is that mothers should not say no to their children because it makes them very sad.

The End

When I finish my story, I look at my desk mate. Pamela is still busy writing. I put my head down on my desk. I knew my birth month wasn't going so well, but I didn't realize how bad it was until now.

I close my eyes and do what I do when

I want something to happen and I'm not sure it's going to. I pretend like I'm at the wish pond on my street, and I make a wish.

I wish that the second week of my birth month will be better than the first week.

I try to draw a picture in my brain of the cookie cake with rainbow writing that I want for my second cake-of-the-week. When I know exactly what it looks like, I pretend to throw a wish pebble in the wish pond.

I sure hope my wish comes true.

HALF-BIRTHDAYS

Grandma says when you're waiting for something to happen, time goes slowly. She says there's a clock fairy that sits on the hands of the clock to slow them down.

The clock fairy must have been sitting on my clock because this week felt like the slowest week of my life. I never thought today would get here.

I sit up in bed and look at my calendar. "Cheeseburger," I say to my cat, "this Saturday is going to be different than last Saturday."

Last Saturday, I was sad, sad, sad. Just thinking about the chocolate cake with fudge frosting that I didn't get makes me feel like staying in bed. But this Saturday, I'm happy, happy, happy. I'm celebrating my birth month with a cookie cake with rainbow writing!

I scoop up Cheeseburger, pop out of bed, and skip into the bathroom.

I open up my hair-thingies drawer and pull out my rainbow ribbon. I put my hair in a ponytail and tie the ribbon around it. When I'm finished, I look in the mirror. "My hair will match the icing on my cookie cake," I tell Cheeseburger.

I tuck her under my arm and skip down

the hall into the kitchen.

Mom smiles when she sees me. "Mallory, I'm glad it's you. Would you like to help me bake a cake?"

Someone should give Mom a T-shirt that says *"Mind Reader."*

"That's exactly what I'd like to do!"

"I was hoping you'd say that," says Mom. She opens up her cookbook and starts taking ingredients from the pantry. Flour, sugar, vanilla, coconut.

I pick up the bag of coconut. I love cookie cake, but I hate coconut. I'm surprised cookie cake has something in it that I hate.

I look at the recipe in Mom's cookbook, and when I do, I get another surprise. "Mom, this isn't a recipe for cookie cake. This is a recipe for coconut cake."

Mom takes eggs and butter from the

refrigerator.

"You know I don't like coconut, so why would you bake a coconut cake for my cake-of-the-week?" I say to Mom.

"Mallory, this cake is for Winnie," says Mom. "We're invited to the Winstons' tonight to celebrate her half-birthday. Mr. Winston asked if I would bake a cake."

This cake wasn't supposed to be for

Winnie! "Mom, why are we celebrating Winnie's birthday, which is half a year away, when my birthday is in less than two weeks?"

Mom puts the eggs and butter down on the counter. "Winnie will be at sleepaway camp on her real birthday, so she wants to celebrate her half-birthday at home."

"Why don't we make two cakes?" I say to Mom. "We can celebrate Winnie's half-birthday and my birth month."

Max walks into the kitchen and grabs a banana. "Enough with the birth month stuff," he says. "It's getting stupid."

I put my hands on my hips. "If you think celebrating my birth month is stupid, I bet you think celebrating Winnie's half-birthday is really stupid."

Max takes a bite of banana. "That's different."

I don't see what's different about it. I march over to where Mom is mixing. "You said I could have a cake-a-week for my birth month, remember?"

Mom stops mixing. "Mallory, I never said you could have a cake-a-week."

"You said it was a sweet idea."

Mom takes a deep breath. She says my name slowly like she has something to tell me and she isn't sure where to start. "Mal-lor-y, I think we've had a misunderstanding. Having a cake is always a fun thing to do, but I didn't mean you could have one every week."

"Can I have one tonight?"

"Tonight is Winnie's night. We're going to the Winstons' house for her celebration." She drops a stick of butter into the mixer. Then she continues talking. "You have a lot to look forward to. Next Friday is your class party. Then, Mary Ann and her mom are coming to visit. And, you're having a skating party."

I start to explain to Mom why she's not being fair, but she gives me a *that's-the-end-of-this-discussion* look. She pours a cup of sugar into the mixer and turns it on.

I go into my room and sit down on my bed with Cheeseburger.

I think about my birth month. It isn't going the way I wanted it to. Just thinking about it gives me a funny feeling . . . and that feeling stays with me all day. I still have it as we walk next door to the Winstons' for Winnie's half-birthday party.

"Welcome," Mr. Winston says to Mom, Dad, Max, and me when he answers the door. "What a beautiful cake," he says to Mom when he sees what she's holding.

I look at the words *Happy Half-Birthday,*

Winnie on the top of the cake. I can't help
wishing they said *Happy Birth Month, Mallory*.

Mr. Winston pats me on the head. "Joey's
in his room. Why don't you go get him
and come to the kitchen. Then the party
can start."

I walk down the hall to Joey's room. His

door is open, so I walk in. "Ready for Winnie's party?"

"Yeah," Joey says. Then he points to a calendar on his wall. "I'm ready for your party too. Just one week and two days till we go skating."

I shrug my shoulders.

"Aren't you excited?"

I don't want Joey to think I'm unexcited to have a party, so I explain. "The thing is, I really didn't want a skating party. I don't even have my own skates."

"You can rent skates at the skating rink," says Joey. He smiles like he has all the answers. "See, no problem."

Joey says "no problem" like my birthday is going to be great. But the thing is, I don't feel like it's going to be great. I don't feel like anything is going the way I wanted it to.

When we walk into the kitchen, balloons and streamers are hanging from the ceiling. There's a sign on the wall that says *Happy Half-Birthday, Winnie!* Two big boxes wrapped in yellow tissue paper are sitting on the counter.

"We have everything Winnie likes tonight. Pizza, spaghetti, and Caesar salad," says Mr. Winston.

Joey points to the boxes on the counter. "Presents too."

Winnie smiles like she's really happy. Usually, she only smiles if somebody else did something dumb. "Dad," she says, "can I open my presents now?"

Mr. Winston laughs. "How about after dinner?"

Everybody takes plates and piles them high with pizza, spaghetti, and salad. I love pizza, spaghetti, and salad, but tonight, I

put just a little of each on my plate.

Joey looks at the single strand of spaghetti on my plate. "Mallory, is that all you want? I thought spaghetti was one of your favorites."

I look down at my plate. "I'm not very hungry."

Joey pretends to feel my forehead. "You're not getting sick are you?"

Joey is not a doctor. I shake my head *no* and move his hand.

"Pre-birthday jitters?" he asks.

I know Joey is trying to be funny and make me laugh. But I don't. I shake my head *no* again.

Mr. Winston looks concerned. "Mallory, is something bothering you?"

I wasn't going to bring this up, but since he asked, I explain. "It's just that tonight, I was supposed to . . ."

Before I can even say the words *celebrate my birth month*, Dad stops me.

"Everything is fine," says Dad. He gives me a *stop-talking-and-start-eating* look. Mom looks at me too, like she can't believe what I was about to say.

I stick my fork into a piece of lettuce and chew my Caesar salad in silence. I feel like nobody, not even Mom and Dad, cares about celebrating my birth month.

After dinner, we sing *Happy Half-Birthday* to Winnie. Even Max, who never sings, sings. Winnie blows out her candles, then she opens her presents.

She gets a new sweater from her dad and a matching hat and gloves from Joey.

She pulls her hat on her head to model it. "I love everything!" says Winnie.

Everyone is smiling.

I try to smile too, but my mouth is

having a hard time cooperating.

"Can we cut the cake now?" asks Winnie.

Mom slices and Joey passes around plates.

I look at Mom. She gives me a slice of coconut cake and a *don't-be-rude* look.

I think about the piece of cookie cake that should be on this plate, and even though I hate coconut cake, I do something I never thought I was going to have to do during my birth month . . . I take a bite.

There's only one thing worse than a birth month that isn't going like you wanted it to . . . and that's a mouthful of coconut.

PARTY POOPED

"MOM! DAD! COME QUICK!" I yell from my bedroom.

I hear Mom and Dad running down the hall. They're in my bedroom in less time than it takes to sneeze.

"Mallory, what's the matter?" asks Dad. He's out of breath.

I hold up a purple turtleneck with fringe and a pink sweater covered in hearts. "Which one do you think I should wear?"

Mom and Dad look at each other, then Dad puts his hands over his heart. "Phew!" he says. "I thought something was wrong."

I put my hands on my hips. "Something is wrong! I can't decide which outfit to wear for my class party today. I don't want to pick the wrong one!"

Mom smiles. "I'm glad to see you're so excited."

I look in the mirror and hold my two outfits up to my face. Then I smile at Mom.

"Of course I'm excited! I just don't know how I'm going to be able to wait until you and Dad get to my classroom this afternoon with the cupcakes."

Dad laughs. "Visions of pink cupcakes will be dancing through your head."

"That's it!" I tell Dad. "You just gave me a great idea!" I stick the purple turtleneck back into my drawer and pull the pink sweater over my head. Then I pull on the matching pink pants. "I'll wear pink, so I match my cupcakes."

"Glad I could help," says Dad. He kisses my forehead. "I've got to go to work, but I'll see you this afternoon."

Mom ruffles my hair. "Hurry," she says. "You don't want to be late for school."

Mom is right. I don't want to miss a minute of what I know will be the best day yet of my birth month.

I go into my bathroom. I tie a big pink bow in my hair and pull a handful of pink stretchy bracelets over my wrist. "Now I'm perfectly pink!" I tell Cheeseburger. I pick up my cat and walk into the kitchen.

Max is already at the breakfast table with Champ. When I walk in, he looks up and laughs. "Did you fall into a bucket of pink paint?"

I take a waffle out of the toaster and sit down at the breakfast table. "For your information, I picked pink on purpose."

Max looks at me like that makes about as much sense as choosing a day-old doughnut. "Why would anybody pick pink on purpose?"

I think about the vanilla cupcakes with strawberry icing that Dad is picking up from the bakery this afternoon. "My class party is today, and I'm wearing pink so I'll match my cupcakes," I tell Max.

Max laughs, and when he does, little bits of waffle fly out of his mouth and land on his plate. "I've heard of eating cupcakes, but I've never heard of matching them."

Champ licks Max's plate.

Mom passes Max a napkin. "Today is a special day for Mallory."

Mom is right. Today is special, and I don't want anything to go wrong. "Can we go over the plan again?" I ask.

Mom nods.

"Dad is picking up the cupcakes from the bakery this afternoon?"

Mom nods again.

"And you're bringing everything else?"

"I've got it all," says Mom. "Don't worry."

But I can't help worrying. So far, my birth month hasn't gone like I had planned, and I don't want anything to mess up my

class party. "Can we check the bag one more time?"

Mom opens the grocery bag with all the party supplies in it. Candles. Matches. *Happy Birthday* plates and napkins. Mom's camera, so she can take pictures for my birth month scrapbook.

"Everything we need to make sure today is the best-school-party-ever is in the bag," Mom says.

On the way to school, I tell Joey how

excited I am. "I don't know how I'm going to be able to wait all day," I say as we walk into Room 310.

Joey looks at his watch. "You actually only have to wait six hours."

Maybe six hours isn't all day, but to me, it feels like it might as well be six years. I can't wait until this afternoon!

Before Mrs. Daily makes everyone sit down, I tell my friends that my parents are bringing birthday cupcakes at the end of the day.

"Oooh, I love cupcakes," squeals Danielle.

"Me too," says Arielle.

"What kind are they?" asks Pamela.

"The yummy kind," I tell Pamela. I want everyone to be surprised when they see my cupcakes.

"Class, please take your seats," says Mrs. Daily. "We have a lot to do today, and we have a birthday party at the end of the day." Mrs. Daily smiles at me, then she writes *Happy Birthday, Mallory* on the chalkboard.

"Mallory's real birthday is on Monday, but since there's no school on Monday, we're going to celebrate today."

Mrs. Daily tells us to open our math books to page 112.

During math, I try to focus on multiplication, but I keep looking at the clock.

Every time I do, the hands remind me of candles, and I think about my class party at the end of the day.

Some school days go by slowly, but today is the slowest ever.

I can hardly wait for 2:30 to get here.

When it finally does, I stop watching the clock and start watching the door. "My parents should be here any minute," I tell Pamela.

"Soon it will be lights, camera, cupcakes!" she says.

I watch the door swing open, and Mom walks in. She walks over to my desk and hugs me. "You have everything," I say looking into the grocery bag in her arms.

"Almost everything," she says smiling. "Dad should be here any minute with the cupcakes."

The door swings open again and Dad walks in. But his hands are empty. "Where are the cupcakes?" I ask when he comes over to my desk.

Dad pats me on the head. "Sweetheart, Mom has the cupcakes."

I look at Dad. "She said you were bringing them."

Dad looks at Mom. "Sherry, you have the cupcakes, right?"

Mom shakes her head. "Harry, you were supposed to stop at the bakery on the way here and pick them up."

"I thought you were bringing everything," says Dad. Mom and Dad start whispering to each other.

If they are playing a birthday joke on me, it's not funny. "Who brought the cupcakes?" I ask softly. I know somebody has to have the cupcakes, because you can't have a party without them.

Dad puts his hands on my shoulders. He has a funny look on his face. "Sweet Potato, I'm afraid Mom and I had a little mix-up."

"Is there a problem?" Mrs. Daily asks.

Mom explains to Mrs. Daily that Dad was supposed to pick up the cupcakes, but he thought she was bringing them.

"You mean no one brought the cupcakes?!?" I say.

Mom and Dad don't say anything, but I know the answer. There are no lights. There are no cameras. THERE ARE NO CUPCAKES!

"Can't Dad go get them?" I ask.

Mrs. Daily looks at me. "Mallory, school ends soon. There's not enough time for your dad to go get the cupcakes and bring them back in time to have a party."

"I've got some mints in my purse," says Mom. "Why don't I pass out mints to everyone, and we can still sing *Happy Birthday?*"

I sit down at my desk. "You can't put a candle in a mint," I say to Mom.

"I've got some potato chips," says Joey.

"You can't stick a candle in a chip, either," I tell him.

"How about half a tuna sandwich from my lunch?" says Pamela. "We could stick a candle in that."

I look down at the floor. I don't want everyone to sing *Happy Birthday* to me over mints or potato chips or tuna fish. I want my pink and white cupcakes.

Mrs. Daily puts her arm around me. "We don't need cupcakes to celebrate your birthday. Class, let's all sing *Happy Birthday* to Mallory."

I try to smile while my class sings. But inside, I don't feel very smiley.

Dad puts his arm around me. "Mallory, Mom and I made a mistake, and we sure are sorry." He hugs me. "I feel like a real party pooper," says Dad.

"Me too," says Mom.

Me three. I feel like my party pooped before it ever popped.

Joey comes over to me. "Hey, at least Mary Ann will be here tonight."

I try to smile. I know Mom and Dad didn't mean to forget the cupcakes. And I know Joey is trying to make me feel better, but so far, my birth month celebration has been a big, fat flop.

At least Joey's right about one thing: Mary Ann is coming tonight. And when she gets here, I just know everything will get better.

It can't get worse.

MALLORY GETS A MAKEOVER

I line up bottles and jars, brushes and combs on my bathroom sink. Then I look at my watch. "Cheeseburger," I say, "we've got a lot to do, and not much time to do it."

Mary Ann and her mom will be here in less than an hour. The Winstons are coming over for a pre-birthday dinner.

Tonight is the official start of my birth weekend. And it's not just a regular birth weekend. There's no school on Monday, so it's a three-day-long birth weekend.

Even though my class party was a flop, I know tonight will be great. And I want to look great. I want to look like I'm turning nine on Monday because on Monday . . . I AM TURNING NINE!!!

I look at Cheeseburger. "Why don't we start with makeup." Mom usually won't let me wear makeup, but she said I could put on a little since tonight is a special occasion.

I brush sparkly peach blush on my cheeks. I coat my lips with shiny pink lip gloss. I even put a dab of shimmery blue shadow on my eyelids. Then I paint my nails with pale yellow polish and blow on them, so they'll dry quickly.

"How do I look?" I ask Cheeseburger.

She purrs. I take that as a good sign. "Now it's time for hair," I say.

I open up my drawer with all my hair thingies in it. I take out a pair of barrettes. I pull back a little hair on each side of my face and clip in the barrettes.

I look in the mirror. This doesn't look like a nine-year-old hairstyle. I rip out the barrettes and pull my hair into a ponytail on top of my head.

But when I look in the mirror, I don't like what I see. "This doesn't even look like an eight-year-old hairstyle," I mumble to Cheeseburger.

I take out the ponytail, fluff up my

bangs, and put a little gel on the ends. I
even try twisting the ends into little curls.
I still don't like what I see.

"Cheeseburger, what I need is a nine-
year-old makeover. Any ideas?" But when
I look at Cheeseburger, she's asleep on top
of the toilet.

I try rubbing my forehead with my
pinkies. That's what I always do when I'm
trying to think of a good idea. But today,
it's not so easy to rub my forehead with my
pinkies, because my forehead is covered up
with bangs.

I try pushing them to the side, but they
fall back down onto my face.

And that's when I get an idea. NOT
being able to rub my forehead gives me a
great idea. What I need is less hair on my
forehead. I stare into the mirror and try to
imagine what I would look like if my bangs

weren't so long.

What I imagine is me, but not eight-year-old me. I see nine-year-old Mallory. I walk over to my desk and get my scissors. "I'm just going to cut a little off the bottom," I say to Cheeseburger when I'm back in the bathroom.

I start on the left side of my forehead and work my way to the right. When I'm finished, I look in the mirror. The left side looks a little longer than the right side.

I cut a little more off the left, just to even it up. But when I'm done, the left side looks a little shorter to me than the right side.

Cutting bangs isn't as easy as I thought it would be.

I nudge Cheeseburger so she'll wake up.

She opens her eyes. "Cheeseburger, I need a second opinion." I point to the right side of my bangs. "Does this side look a

little shorter to you?"

Cheeseburger purrs. I take that as a *yes*.
I snip some hair off the bottom of the right
side of my bangs.

Now the right side looks MUCH shorter
than the left, and I don't need a second
opinion to know that.

I pull the left side of my bangs into a
chunk and start snipping.

When I'm finished, I look in the mirror.

What I would like to see are bangs that are even on the left side and the right side. But what I see are NO bangs on the left side.

"CHEESEBURGER!" I scream. "LOOK AT MY HAIR!"

Cheeseburger jumps when I scream, and she looks at me. I can tell by the way she's looking that she thinks something is wrong.

I can't have bangs on one side and not the other. I grab the scissors and snip off the bangs on the right side of my forehead to try to make things even.

When I'm finished, I look in the mirror. Now I have NO bangs on either side! I don't look like *nine-year-old* Mallory. I look like a Ping-Pong ball. I reach up to feel the spot where my bangs used to be. It feels prickly.

"This is awful!" I tell Cheeseburger. I can't believe I cut my bangs off . . . right when Mary Ann is coming to town, right

before my birthday.

I can feel my eyes filling up with tears.

"Oh, Cheeseburger!" I moan. "What am I going to do?"

But Cheeseburger just stares at the pile of hair on the floor that used to be my bangs.

"Mary Ann is going to be here any minute. I don't want anyone to see me like this, not even my best friend," I tell Cheeseburger. Tears roll down my cheeks.

There's only one thing I can do. I go into my bedroom and lock the door.

I'm staying in my room forever . . . or at least until my bangs grow out. I try to think how long it will take.

One time when I got a haircut, the haircutter told me that hair grows one-half an inch a month. I try to measure my forehead with my index finger. It's about two inches long, which means I'll be stuck in my room for at least four months.

If I'm stuck in here for that long, I could starve! I'm hungry already.

"Mallory!" Mom yells from the kitchen. "Mary Ann is here."

I pull aside my curtains and look outside. Mary Ann's mom's van is in the driveway. I see the Winstons walking over. I close my curtains. I don't want any of them to see me.

I hear everyone inside my house.

"Mallory!" Mom calls my name again.

I hear footsteps running down the hall.

"Mallory! Open up! I'm here! " says a familiar voice on the other side of my door.

I reach up and rub my prickly spot. I can't let Mary Ann see me like this.

"Mallory? Are you in there?"

I don't answer. I hear Mary Ann going

back down the hall.

Then I hear more footsteps and voices coming toward my room. "Mallory, open up."

"I can't come out," I tell Dad.

"Why not?" Dad sounds concerned.

"I can't tell you why, but trust me, I can't."

"She has to come out," Mary Ann says to Dad.

"C'mon," says Dad. "Everyone's here. Mary Ann, Joey, Winnie. It's time for your pre-birthday dinner."

"I'm not coming out," I tell Dad. "Not now. Not for a long time."

"Mallory," says Dad. "I'm going to count to three, and I want you to open this door."

Dad counts, but I don't open the door.

"Mallory Louise McDonald, open this door this instant!" says Dad.

I don't.

"I think your dad went to get your mom," says Mary Ann.

She's right. Mom is at my door in less time than it takes to cut off your bangs. "Mallory, what's wrong? You need to come out of your room. We want to start dinner, and we can't start without you."

I don't answer Mom. I just curl up on my bed next to Cheeseburger.

"Mallory, I'm not going to ask again. You need to come out of your room now, and if you don't, we're starting without you."

I think about the cheeseburgers Dad is making on the grill. I think about the cupcakes and ice cream Mom is serving for dessert. I think about how much fun it would be to celebrate my birthday with my family and friends.

Then I think about my hair. I can just hear what Max would say if he saw me

without bangs. *If you look up the word ugly in the dictionary, you'd see Mallory's picture next to it.*

"Start without me," I tell Mom.

I pull Cheeseburger close to me. "It's just you and me," I tell her, "for the next four months."

A PAJAMA
PARTY

Mary Ann bangs on my door. "C'mon," she says. "Open up. I've been here for two hours, and I haven't even seen you yet."

I want to see my best friend, but I don't want her to see me. "I'm not opening my door," I tell Mary Ann.

"Why not?" she asks.

"I can't tell you why not."

"But I'm your best friend," says Mary Ann. "You can tell me anything. We came here to celebrate your birthday, and I can't celebrate if I can't see you!"

"Mallory, open up right now," says Dad. I watch my doorknob rattle.

I know I can't stay locked in my room forever. Mary Ann is my best friend, and she did come to celebrate my birthday. I take my snow hat out of the closet and pull it down over my forehead. I open my door.

When I do, Mom, Dad, Max, Mary Ann, and her mom are all standing there.

They walk into my room. "What's going on?" asks Mom. She looks suspicious.

Mary Ann gives me a hug. "Your pre-birthday dinner wasn't much fun without you." Then she gets a funny look on her face. "Why are you wearing your hat inside?"

Before I can stop her, Mary Ann reaches up and pulls my hat off my head.

"MALLORY?" Mom says my name like she's not sure she recognizes me.

Mary Ann puts her hands on her cheeks. "Mallory, where are your bangs?"

I cover my forehead with one hand and

point toward my bathroom with the other. "On the floor in there," I say.

Max laughs. "I never thought I'd say this, but they looked better on than off."

"Max, that's enough." Mom gives Max a sharp look. Then she walks over to me and inspects what's left of my hair. "Honey, why did you cut your bangs?" Mom asks.

I explain that my makeover didn't turn out like I thought it would. When I'm finished talking, Mom puts her arm around me. "It's really not a big deal. Your hair will grow back before you know it."

Dad smiles at me. "Just think of all the money we'll save on shampoo."

I know Dad is trying to make me laugh, but I'm not in the mood for jokes.

"I think you look cute and grown up." Mary Ann's mom puts one arm around me and the other around Mary Ann. "Now why don't we get out of here and let you two catch up with each other."

I might have lost my bangs, but at least I still have my best friend. "That sounds great," I say.

After everyone leaves, I look at Mary Ann. "What am I going to do?"

"We're going to find a new hairstyle for you," says Mary Ann.

"Do you really think we can?"

Mary Ann nods. "Of course we can!"

I hug her. "You're the best, best, best friend in the whole wide world."

Mary Ann grins. "Let's put on our pajamas first, and we'll have a *Find-a-New-Hairstyle-for-Mallory* pajama party."

Now it's my turn to grin. Mary Ann knows I love pajama parties!

Mary Ann pulls her penguin pajamas out of her suitcase. I put on my matching ones,

then scoop up Cheeseburger and follow
Mary Ann into the bathroom.

She opens my hair-thingies drawer and
pulls out handfuls of ribbons, headbands,
and clips. "We're going to have to
experiment until we find the right hairstyle
for you." Mary Ann picks up a purple
ribbon and ties it into a
big bow on the front of
my head.

I look in the mirror,
but when I see myself,
I shut my eyes. "I look
like an overgrown baby,"
I tell Mary Ann.

Mary Ann looks at
my reflection in the mirror, then unties the
bow. I open one eye and watch while she
pins in butterfly clips all over the front of
my head.

"What do you think?" asks Mary Ann.

I look in the mirror. "I think I look like the butterfly exhibit at the zoo."

"Hmmm," says Mary Ann. "I see what you mean." She takes the clips out. "Let's try this." She pushes a thick striped headband over the front of my head.

I look in the mirror and smile. "I like it!"

Cheeseburger purrs. "I think Cheeseburger likes it too," says Mary Ann. She smiles. "You look cute with or without bangs," she says.

When I cut off my bangs, I thought tonight would be a total disaster, but it turned out OK. I throw my arms around Mary Ann. "This has been our best pajama party ever."

Mary Ann nods, like she agrees.

"We'll have to go headband shopping," I say to Mary Ann. I start thinking about all my different outfits. "I'll need a red one and a purple one and a green one and a blue one. Maybe we'll go tomorrow," I say.

Mary Ann grins. "I can't believe I forgot to tell you what's happening tomorrow."

I try to think what could be happening tomorrow. Tomorrow is Saturday. My skating party isn't until Monday. Maybe Mom planned something else on Saturday for my birth month celebration.

"Are you sure it's OK to tell me?" I ask Mary Ann. "I wouldn't want to spoil any surprises."

Mary Ann smiles even bigger than when she found the perfect hairstyle for me. "I think you'll be surprised when you hear this. Tonight at dinner, my mom and Joey's dad sat next to each other."

I shrug my shoulders. "What's the big deal about them sitting next to each other?"

"I think they liked sitting next to each other, because tomorrow night, they're going out on a date. Isn't that great?" squeals Mary Ann.

I rub my ear. "I guess so," I say.

"Think about it," says Mary Ann. "Joey's mom died, so Joey's dad is all alone. And since my parents are divorced, my mom is all alone." Mary Ann smiles. "If you ask me, they make the perfect pair."

If you ask me, there is nothing perfect about it.

If Mary Ann's mom and Joey's dad go out on a date, they might fall in love.

If they fall in love, they might decide to get married.

If they get married, Mary Ann and Joey

will become step-brother and sister.

If they become step-brother and sister, they will do all kinds of things, like live in the same house together, and eat all their meals together, and go on family vacations together. And they will do all these things . . . WITHOUT ME!

Mary Ann taps me on the head. "Isn't it so, so, so great that my mom and Joey's dad are going out on a date?"

I nod my head yes, that I do think it is great. But I don't think it's great at all. In fact, I think it is terrible, even worse than cutting off my bangs. Mary Ann and her mom came to see me on my birthday. They didn't come so Mary Ann's mom could go out on a date with Joey's dad.

Mary Ann and I get into bed, and she reaches up and turns off the light. "Watch out for bedbugs!" says Mary Ann.

I say it back, because that's what we always say to each other at pajama parties. But as I put my head on my pillow, I don't think about bedbugs. I think about our pajama party, and all I can think is that the best-pajama-party-ever just turned into the worst-pajama-party-ever.

HIGHS AND WOES

"Who wants pizza, and who wants . . . " Crystal, our Saturday-night babysitter, looks around the kitchen, then finishes her sentence. "Pizza?" She laughs at her joke. She knows all there is to pick from is pizza.

"I'll have the . . . " Joey pretends to consider his choices. "Pizza," he says in a funny voice. Then he cracks up.

"Hmmm," says Mary Ann, like she can't decide what she wants. "I think I'll have . . . pizza too." She laughs along with Joey.

Even Winnie and Max smile like they think the whole pizza thing is funny.

"Everyone sure is in a good mood tonight," says Crystal.

Make that *almost* everyone.

I must be the only kid on Wish Pond Road who is not in a good mood. I pull my headband down over my forehead.

"Guess who's going out on a date tonight?" Joey says to Crystal.

Crystal puts a slice of pizza on a paper plate. "Give me a hint."

"He lives in my house. He's bald. And he's not my grandfather," says Joey.

Crystal laughs. "Gee, this is a tough one. I would say your dad, but he never goes out on dates."

"He is tonight," says Mary Ann. "He's going out with my mom!"

Crystal pretends like she's looking into a crystal ball. "I see a fancy restaurant. I see flowers. I see candles. I see true love!"

Crystal thinks she is a fortune-teller.

Sometimes, I think she knows what she's

talking about. But not this time. She can't know that Joey's dad and Mary Ann's mom are going to fall in love. She just met Mary Ann and her mom tonight for the first time.

I take a slice of pizza out of the box, go into the living room, and sit down on the couch with Cheeseburger.

Maybe Mary Ann, Joey, Winnie, Max, and even Crystal are happy about Mary Ann's mom and Joey's dad going out on a date, but I'm not.

My mom and Mary Ann's mom spent the whole day talking about it.

What should Mary Ann's mom wear? How should she do her hair? What color should she paint her nails?

Dad was on the phone all afternoon trying to make a reservation at a restaurant.

Did they want French? Or maybe

Italian? Should they go at seven or at eight?

Mary Ann and Joey and Winnie talked all day about their parents going out.

What if they like each other? What if they really, really, really like each other?

All anybody talked about today was "The Date." But if you ask me, they were talking about the wrong date. The date they should have been talking about is my birth date. It seems like everyone around here has forgotten that I'm turning nine in two days.

Especially Mary Ann! She came here to celebrate my birthday, and I think she has forgotten that I'm even having one.

I take a bite of pizza. I hear everyone in the kitchen laughing. I rub Cheeseburger's back. "I guess it's just you and me," I say to my cat.

"Hey," says Crystal. She sits down beside me. "Why the gloomy face?"

I shrug my shoulders and take another bite of pizza.

Crystal looks at me, then she pretends to look into her crystal ball again.

But I don't give her a chance to predict my future. "It's like this," I explain to Crystal. "My birthday is on Monday. This is my birthday weekend and not one single thing is going the way it's supposed to."

Crystal starts to say something, but I don't let her.

"And to make matters worse, everyone is having a good time. Everyone except for one person, and that one person is ME!"

"Mallory," Crystal says. But I stop her. I pull my headband down on my forehead and point to the spot where my bangs used to be.

Crystal looks me in the eye. "Mallory,

your bangs will grow. And I don't need a crystal ball to tell me what's wrong with you. What you have is a bad case of highs and woes."

I'm not sure I want to know, but I ask anyway. "What are highs and woes?"

"Think of it like this," Crystal explains. "Sometimes when you feel good, you feel like you're high up in the air. It seems like your feet are barely touching the ground, and your head is way up in the clouds. And sometimes, when you feel bad, you feel low, like your whole body is crawling around in the dirt."

Sometimes I think Crystal is the weirdest babysitter in Fern Falls. "Well, wouldn't that be called *highs and lows,* not *highs and woes?*" I ask Crystal.

Crystal shakes her head, like she's an old, wise woman who's about to explain something to me. "You have to understand the difference between *lows* and *woes*."

I raise an eyebrow. Crystal is going to tell me the difference between *lows* and *woes*, whether I want to know or not.

"*Lows* are when you feel badly about something. But *woes* are different. *Woes* are when you feel badly about something, and everybody else feels good about it, which makes you feel even worse." Crystal gets a serious look on her face. "Do you understand what I'm saying?"

I rub my forehead. "I guess," I mumble without looking up. Somehow listening to Crystal tell me I have *woes* makes me feel even worse.

Crystal puts her arm around me. "Cheer up, Mal," she says.

"I'll try," I tell Crystal.

But I feel woe . . . as woe as you can go.

BIRTHDAY WISHES

I run my fingers through the pebbles on the edge of the wish pond. I see white and gray pebbles. What I don't see are shiny, little black pebbles, otherwise known as wish pebbles.

When I moved to Wish Pond Road, Joey told me that when you find a wish pebble and throw it into the wish pond, your wish is supposed to come true.

It sounds simple, but wish pebbles are hard to find, especially when you need one. And right now, I need one.

I pick up the closest thing I can find that looks like a wish pebble. I close my eyes and start to make a wish. But when I do, my wish turns into a wish list.

I wish my birth month had gone like I had planned it to.

I wish I hadn't cut off my bangs.

I wish Mary Ann's mom and Joey's dad hadn't gone out on a date.

I wish they won't go out on another one.

I start to throw my stone in the wish pond, then I think about my skating party tomorrow. Even though my wish list is long, I add another one to it.

I wish Mom had planned a surprise party for me. I can't help thinking about how much fun it would be to walk into a party and be super surprised.

I squeeze the stone in the palm of my hand. I'm about to throw it in the wish pond when I hear someone sit down beside me. I open one eye. It's Dad. "How did you know I was here?" I ask him.

Dad sits down beside me. "I heard the front door open. Mom, Max, Mary Ann, her mom, Champ, and Cheeseburger were all asleep in their beds. The only one I couldn't find was you. I thought you might be out here."

I cross my arms.

"What are you doing out here by yourself so early in the morning?"

"Making wishes," I tell Dad.

Dad picks up a stone and throws it into the pond. "Feel like talking about what you're wishing for?"

I look down at the pebble in my hand. "If I tell, my wishes might not come true."

"Sometimes talking about things is better than wishing for them," says Dad.

I close my fingers around the pebble in my hand. "I don't know where to start."

"How about the beginning?" says Dad.

I think about my wish list. My long, long, long wish list. Then I take a deep breath and start. "I worked so hard to plan the perfect birth month celebration," I tell Dad. "And nothing happened like it was supposed to."

"Mallory, I know you expected things to happen a certain way during your birth

month, and they didn't. I know that's disappointing."

"But that's not all." I reach up and feel my forehead. "I was just trying to look like a nine-year-old, and look what happened to my hair."

Dad puts his arm around me. "Sweet Potato, it'll grow back."

Then I tell Dad how scared I am about Mary Ann's mom and Joey's dad liking each other. "I wish they hadn't gone out on a date."

"But they did," says Dad. "And you can't change that."

"Did they have a good time?" I cross my toes and hope Dad says *no*.

But he nods his head *yes*. "They had a very nice time together," says Dad.

This is not what I wanted to hear.

"Do you think they'll go out again?" I ask.

Dad looks down at me. "Yes, I do."

I kick my foot against a pile of rocks on the side of the wish pond. "What if they fall in love and get married, and Mary Ann and Joey become brother and sister, and they're together all the time without me?"

"Sweet Potato, there are some things you can control, and some things you can't. And when you can't control something, you just have to accept it."

Dad tilts my face up so I'm looking at him. "Do you understand what I'm trying to tell you?"

I shake my head no. I'm not sure I do.

"Mallory, things didn't happen the way you expected them to. You might wish that things could have been different, but you can't change what happened."

I think about what Dad said. I can't change what happened during my birth

month. I can't make my bangs reappear.
I can't do anything about the fact that
Mary Ann's mom and Joey's dad went out
on a date, and that they might go out on
another one.

But there is something I *can* change.
"Thanks Dad, you gave me a great idea!"

Dad smiles at me. "Glad I could help."

I stand up and start to go home. Then
I stop.

I squeeze the rock in my hand, then
throw it into the wish pond. *I wish my
birthday party will be the best surprise party
in the whole world.*

And I'm planning to make sure that it is.

MALLORY ON HER OWN

"You want to plan your own surprise party?"

"No," I explain to Mary Ann. "I want you to plan it." I sit down on the bed next to her. "And I'll be your assistant."

Mary Ann looks confused. "But if you're my assistant, everybody will know that you know about the surprise."

"That's the thing," I whisper to Mary Ann. "No one will know I'm your assistant . . . no one but you."

Mary Ann winks at me. "I get it. You're going to be my *secret* assistant."

"Exactly!" I say. Then I stop to think for a minute. "There's just one more problem. How are you going to tell my mom that you're planning a surprise party when she's already planned a skating party?"

"Simple," says Mary Ann. "I'll tell her that you really want a surprise party and as your lifelong best friend, I want to make one for you."

Mary Ann makes it sound simple, but I'm not sure it will be. "Don't you think my mom will be upset when she finds out I don't want to have the party she planned?"

Mary Ann shrugs. "I'm sure she'll understand when I explain it to her."

I'm not so sure Mom will understand. She didn't understand when I told her I wanted to celebrate my birth month. She didn't understand when I said I wanted to get my ears pierced. I'm not sure she'll understand this either.

Mary Ann leans over and taps me on the head with a pencil. "Earth to Mallory. We've got a lot to do to plan a surprise party before tomorrow."

She closes the door to my room and sits down at my desk. "Let's make a list of everything we need."

I sit down on my bed with Cheeseburger. Mary Ann starts writing.

"Invitations," says Mary Ann. "We need to tell everybody that your party has changed from a skating party to a surprise party."

"We can make our own." I show Mary

Ann a picture in a magazine of party invitations shaped like paper fans.

Mary Ann claps her hands together when she sees it. "They'll be so cute!"

I nod. They will be cute, but there's a problem. "How will we get them to people in time for the party?"

Mary Ann rubs her chin. "Joey can deliver them for us."

"Now, let's talk about food," says Mary Ann.

"I can make peanut butter and marshmallow sandwiches and lemonade," I say.

"You better let me make them," says Mary Ann. "You don't want anyone to see you making your own party food."

Mary Ann is right. I don't want to spoil my own surprise. "But we still need a cake," I remind her. "Do you know how to bake a cake?"

Mary Ann scratches her head. "Your mom will bring the cake. When I tell her about the party, I'll remind her to bring the cake." Mary Ann looks down at the piece of paper in her lap. "What about party favors?"

I reach over and open the drawer to my nightstand.

I take out a bookmark with a big *M* on it. "We can make bookmarks with everyone's initials on them, and then decorate them with glitter and bows."

"Great idea!" says Mary Ann. "There's just one thing left to do."

"What's that?" I ask.

Mary Ann lowers her voice. "We have to figure out how we're going to surprise you."

I think for a minute. Figuring out how to surprise myself is harder than making invitations and party favors.

I snap my fingers. "I've got it. I'll pretend like I'm getting ready for my skating party. When it's time to go, I'll walk into the living room in my skating clothes and you'll have everybody waiting there to surprise me."

"Perfect!" says Mary Ann. She looks at her watch. "We better get busy or we won't get everything done by tomorrow. I'll go talk to your mom and Joey. You start folding fans."

Mary Ann leaves my room. I reach into my drawer, take out thick sheets of construction paper, and start folding.

Part of me can't wait to be surprised. But part of me feels like planning my own surprise party might not be such a good idea. I hope Mom isn't upset when Mary Ann talks to her.

I keep folding fans. When Mary Ann comes back into my room, my bed is covered with colorful fans. "Wow!" says Mary Ann. "These look great."

"Now all we have to do is write the party information on them, decorate them, and tie ribbons through the bottoms of them," I tell her.

"Joey is ready to deliver them," says

Mary Ann. "And your mom is bringing the cake."

I look up. "Did my mom seem upset when you told her about the party?"

Mary Ann ties a ribbon through the bottom of a fan. "She didn't say she was."

I sprinkle glitter across a yellow fan. Just because Mom didn't say she was upset doesn't mean she's not. I really hope she understands that I want to have a surprise party, and I hope she's OK with that.

When we're finished with the invitations, Mary Ann takes them next door to Joey.

When she comes back, Mary Ann and I start on the bookmarks. We work all morning until Mom knocks on my door. "Time for lunch, girls."

"Remember," I whisper to Mary Ann, "not a word about this to my mom. I don't want her to know I'm in on this."

Mary Ann holds up two fingers like she's making a promise. "It's our secret."

After lunch, Mary Ann and I go back to making bookmarks. "Do you think we'll ever finish?" I ask her.

"Maybe you should finish in here," says Mary Ann. "I'll go make the lemonade and sandwiches." Mary Ann winks at me. "I'll tell your mom you're taking a nap."

By the time Mary Ann and I get ready for bed, we are both tired from all the party planning. "Thanks for everything," I tell Mary Ann as we put on our matching yellow peace-sign pajamas. "I thought I would have to plan my party on my own. But I should have known I could count on you."

Mary Ann smiles at me. "I think this will be the best surprise ever." She turns off the light.

I try to go to sleep, but something is bothering me. I turn the light back on.

Mary Ann sits up. "What's the matter?"

"We forgot something," I tell her.

Mary Ann shakes her head. "We have invitations, favors, and food."

"Clothes!" I say to Mary Ann. "I'm the party girl and I need just the right outfit to

look like I'm going skating."

"Hmmm." Mary Ann looks at me. "Why don't you wear something yellow."

"Good idea," I say to Mary Ann. I get my yellow jeans and matching sweater out of my closet. "Yellow is a perfect party color."

Mary Ann nods, like she agrees. "Watch out for bedbugs!" she says.

"You too," I say. But I'm so tired from all our party planning that I don't think my eyes can stay open long enough to look for bedbugs. I turn out the light and put my head down on the pillow.

"Cheeseburger," I whisper, "I can't wait to be surprised."

SURPRISES!

"Mallory, wake up!"

For a minute, I think I'm being attacked by bedbugs. But when I open my eyes, it's just Mom. "What's the matter?" I ask her.

"Do you know what day it is today?" she asks me.

I have to think for a minute. "Monday?"

"It's Monday," says Mom. "But do you know why this Monday is different than all other Mondays?"

I roll over and look at the clock on my nightstand. It's so early!

"Mom, on all other Mondays, we have school, but today we don't. What's so important about this Monday that you needed to wake me up so early?"

"I think you'll be very excited when you hear what I have to say." Mom sits down on the bed beside me. "Today is your birthday, and I have a surprise for you!"

I think about the surprise party I'm having this afternoon. "A surprise?" I ask Mom.

"Why don't I show you," she says. Mom ties a bandanna around my eyes, then helps me out of bed. I can feel her leading me down the hall.

"Where are we going?" I ask. I can't imagine where she would be taking me so early in the morning in my pajamas.

Mom stops walking. "Would you like to see your surprise?"

I nod. Mom unties the bandanna. When she takes it off, I am surprised . . . VERY SURPRISED!

"HAPPY BIRTHDAY, MALLORY!" shout my friends and my family.

Mom puts a party hat on my head. I look around the living room and can't believe what I'm seeing! Dad, Max, Mary Ann, her mom, Joey, Winnie, Mr. Winston, Crystal, Pamela, and all my friends from school are there . . . and they're all in their pajamas and robes and slippers! Even Champ and Cheeseburger have on little matching nightcaps.

"What's going on?" I ask.

Mom grins. "It's a surprise pajama party for you! We all know how much you love pajama parties."

"And surprise parties!" says Mary Ann.

"But what about my skating party?"

Mom gives me a big hug. "There never was a skating party."

I can't believe it! "There never was a skating party?"

Mom shakes her head. "Dad and I wanted to make sure you would be really surprised." I am really surprised *and* really confused.

"What about the party Mary Ann and I planned? What happened to the invitations we made?" I look at Joey. "The ones you delivered yesterday?"

Joey smiles. "I delivered the

invitations . . . to your mom."

"And I hid them in the kitchen," Mom says.

I can't believe it. "You knew about this?" I say to Joey.

He grins. "I can be a very good secret keeper."

And there's another good secret keeper too. I look at Mary Ann. "You knew about this and spent the whole day yesterday helping me make invitations and bookmarks and sandwiches. You didn't say a word."

"Joey and I didn't want to spoil the real surprise. We were your mom's assistants." She winks at me. "Her secret assistants."

I throw my arms around Mary Ann and Joey. "You're the best friends a girl could have."

And then I look at all my friends. "You all knew about this and nobody said a word?"

Max smiles. "I guess we're all good secret keepers."

Mary Ann giggles. "Look around."

A sign on the wall says, *Happy Birthday, Mallory!* Streamers and balloons hang from the ceiling. There's a big pile of presents in the corner.

The dining room table is covered with all my favorite breakfast foods: doughnuts and hot chocolate with mini-marshmallows, even the platter of peanut butter and marshmallow sandwiches that Mary Ann made.

I pick one up and take a bite. "Mmmmm."

"Don't eat too many sandwiches," says Mom. "You need to save room for cake." Dad carries in a tray with the biggest ice cream cake on it that I've ever seen.

"It's the cake-of-the-year," says Dad.

He puts the cake down on the table and lights the candles. Everybody sings *Happy Birthday*.

"Make a wish," says Mom.

I look at Dad, and we smile at each other. Yesterday at the wish pond, I wished for the best surprise party in the whole world. I close my eyes and blow out my

candles. I feel like my wish is coming true.

Mom cuts the cake and Mary Ann's mom passes around plates.

I take a bite. "Mmmm! Cookies and cream for breakfast is my new favorite."

Dad laughs. "Ice cream for breakfast on birthdays only!"

"Time for games," says Mom when everybody finishes their cake.

We play *Pin the Slippers on the Sheep.* It's like *Pin the Tail on the Donkey,* but you have to pin the slippers onto the sheep's feet.

Mom blindfolds Mary Ann and spins her around in a circle. Mary Ann walks toward the wall and pins the slippers on the sheep's nose.

When it's Joey's turn, he doesn't do much better. He pins the slippers on the sheep's ear, and Pamela pins them on his stomach.

Finally, Max pins the slippers in the right

place . . . on the sheep's feet. Mom gives him a pair of fuzzy yellow slippers as a prize.

Max looks at the slippers like touching them could give him a bad disease. "The birthday girl can have these." He hands me the slippers.

I slip them on my feet. "They look perfect with my pj's!"

I give Max a hug. "You're the best brother a girl could have."

Max rolls his eyes. "On your birthday, only!"

When we finish playing *Pin the Slippers on the Sheep,* Mom holds up a glass jar of jelly beans. "Who wants to play *Guess the Number of Jelly Beans in the Jar?*"

I look at the jar of jelly beans in Mom's

hands. Then I look at the pile of presents.
It's hard to focus on jelly beans when
they're near a pile of presents.

Pamela looks at me. "I think the only
game Mallory wants to play is called *Open
the Presents!*"

I laugh. Pamela knows me really well.
Then I give her a hug. "You're the best
desk mate in all of Fern Falls!"

Mom piles all the boxes on the living
room floor, and everybody sits in a circle
around me.

"Open this one first," says Danielle. "It's
from Arielle and me."

I open a big pink box filled with makeup.
"It's a makeover kit," says Danielle. "It's
what you need if you want a new look."

I thank Danielle and Arielle, but I give
Mary Ann a secret smile. I've had enough
new looks to last me for a while.

I keep opening presents. Mary Ann gives
me a ninth birthday scrapbook. It has nine
hearts on the cover. "One for each year,"
says Mary Ann.

"I love it!" I tell her.

Joey and Winnie give me a new pair of
roller blades. "Now you have your own
skates," says Joey. "And they're purple,"
says Winnie.

"Wow! I can't believe you got me

these!" I take off my fuzzy yellow slippers and try on my new roller blades.

"Now we can go skating," says Joey.

I grin. "Sounds like fun."

I keep opening presents.

Pamela gives me a glow-in-the-dark paper weight. Crystal gives me a days-of-the-week set of headbands.

Mom and Dad give me new pajamas with birthday cakes all over them. "You can celebrate your birthday every time you wear these," says Dad.

Then Max hands me a box. It's big, but it's not heavy. When I shake it, it doesn't make a sound. "I can't imagine what's in here," I say to my brother.

"It's not really for you," says Max. "But I think you'll like it."

Now, I'm really curious. I rip off the wrapping paper and open the box. Inside,

there's a new cat bed for Cheeseburger . . .
and it matches my bed!

"I love it!" I say to Max. I try to hug him.
He ducks, so I miss. But he smiles at me.

"I hope you have a great year!" says Max.

Mom passes out the party favors she
bought. "Mini flashlights," she says, "so
you can read in your pajamas in bed."

Then Mary Ann gives everyone the
bookmarks we made.

After all of the guests have gone, Mom
picks up the tray with the leftover birthday
cake on it. "Did you like your party?" she
asks me.

I scratch my head, like I have to think
hard to answer the question she just
asked me. "Well, it wasn't exactly what I
expected."

Dad looks concerned. "Sometimes," he
says, "you don't get what you expected."

I stop scratching and start smiling. "And sometimes, what you get is even better than what you expected."

Mom puts the cake down. She and Dad both smile.

I hug them both. "Mom, Dad, thanks so much for everything. I loved my party."

"Surprises are fun," says Dad.

I smile at my parents. "Especially when you're really surprised."

"Speaking of surprises," says Dad. "There's another one, and I think I hear it outside."

I run to the front window. Grandma's car is pulling into our driveway. "Grandma!" I scream.

Everyone follows me outside.

When Grandma gets out of her car, I fling myself around her. "I can't believe it! You're what you sent for my birthday!"

Grandma hugs me so hard she crushes my party hat. "I didn't wear pajamas, but I did bring your present . . . in person!" She hands me a box wrapped in purple tissue paper.

I shake the box, but it doesn't make a sound. I rip off the paper and open the lid. Inside, there's a pillow that has the number nine inside a big heart.

I hug my pillow. "It's perfect," I tell Grandma. "I've only been nine for a few minutes, but I love it already! It's definitely full of surprises." I take a deep breath and try to straighten my mashed party hat. "I never thought I'd say this, but I think I've had enough surprises for one day."

Everyone laughs. Then Mary Ann's mom comes over to me. "Actually," she says, "I have one more." She hands me a small box.

I think about my new scrapbook. "But Mary Ann already gave me a present."

"This one's from me," says Mary Ann's mom. "And I think you'll really like it."

I clutch the small box in my hands. When I shake it, something rattles. I don't know what's inside, but I can't wait to find out.

THE REST OF THE HOLE STORY

When I get to school, I hand Mrs. Daily a sheet of paper. "You didn't ask me to write this, but I thought you might like reading it."

"I'm always proud of my students when they do extra work," says Mrs. Daily. Then she smiles at me. "And I can't wait to read the rest of the story!"

The Rest of the Hole Story
by Mallory McDonald
N.T.R. (No Tissues Required)

I know you must remember our
story, which ended when the heroine
was wiping away her tears because
her mother refused to grant her one,
actually two, small requests she made
on her ninth birthday.

I'm sure you can't forget that whole
you-have-to-wait-until-you're-twelve-
to-get-your-ears-pierced speech.

Well, after the girl was forced to
listen to that speech, she went to her
room. Actually, she was sent there.

She made a wish for a miracle
to happen, and to her surprise
and amazement, it did! Her fairy
godmother (actually her lifelong best

friend's mother) gave her a pair of earrings for her birthday.

Of course, the little girl gave them right back and said she didn't need them because her mother wouldn't let her get her ears pierced.

But the girl's fairy godmother just smiled and told her that she explained to the girl's mother that waiting until you're twelve to get your ears pierced, especially when you've just cut off your bangs, didn't seem necessary.

And the girl's mother agreed!!! (I hope you didn't faint when you read this!)

So the fairy godmother drove the girl and the girl's best friend to the mall. (Unfortunately, they had to go in a minivan, not in a golden coach, but what happened next was so exciting, the girl didn't care.)

When she got to the mall, she got her ears pierced!

And everybody lived happily ever after. Especially the girl.

The End

P.S. In most fairy tales, the heroine falls in love with a handsome prince, but in this one, the fairy godmother falls for the man next door. At first, the heroine was pretty upset about this. She was worried about what it meant for her future. But her fairy godmother told the heroine to stop worrying about the future and start picking out earrings. And that's exactly what the heroine did. She picked out heart-shaped earrings and so did her best friend. They vowed to always wear matching earrings.

MALLORY'S PARTY PLANNING KIT

Birthdays are a big deal! Here are some things you can do to make your birthday party extra special!

INVITATIONS

You can make your own invitations shaped like fans. Just follow these four simple steps:

Step 1: Fold a piece of paper into the shape of a fan.

Step 2: On the folds of the paper, write the time, date, and place of your party.

Step 3: Decorate your invitations with paint, markers, and stickers.

Step 4: Deliver your invitations to your friends!

PARTY FAVORS

Handmade bookmarks are super cool. Just cut out paper in the shape of a bookmark. Then draw each guest's initial on the bookmark. Decorate the bookmarks with ribbons and glitter. Every time your friends open their books, they will remember your great party.

THANK-YOU NOTES

Don't forget the thank-you notes! I think the *fill-in-the-blank* ones are the best. You can decorate them so they match your invitations. Here's what mine looked like:

Dear (person's name you're thanking goes here),

Thank you so, so, so much for the super (fill in the gift you received) that you gave me! I really, really, really love it! I am so, so, so glad you could come to my party.

Thanks again! Extra big huge hugs and kisses!

(Just sign your name)

P.S. (I always put a P.S.! It gives you a chance to say something nice about the gift!)

And if you're thinking that writing thank-you notes isn't as much fun as other activities (like getting presents), you and I think a lot alike! But you have to do it. And you have to do it pretty soon after your party, or your mother (if she's anything like mine) will start saying: *"(Fill in your name here!), have you written those notes yet?"*

Trust me, you don't want your mom to start saying that!

Well, I hope you like some of these ideas, and I hope when your birthday rolls around it is super special! I know mine was.

I'm already thinking about my next birthday. I know it's a year away, but I'm turning ten, which is a VERY big deal!

I just love birthdays! Don't you?

Text copyright © 2005 by Laurie B. Friedman
Illustrations copyright © 2005 by Tamara Schmitz

Darby Creek
A division of Lerner Publishing Group, Inc.
241 First Avenue North
Minneapolis, MN 55401 USA

For reading levels and more information, look up this title at www.lernerbooks.com.

Library of Congress Cataloging-in-Publication Data

Friedman, Laurie B.,
    Happy birthday, mallory! / by Laurie Friedman ; illustrations by Tamara Schmitz.
        p.   cm.
    Summary: After a difficult year, mallory plans a month-long celebration of her ninth
birthday in hopes that her next year will be wonderful.
    ISBN 978-1-57505-823-8 (lib. bdg. : alk. paper)
    ISBN 978-0-8225-6297-9 (eBook)
    [1. Birthdays—Fiction.] I. Schmitz, Tamara, ill. II. Title.
PZ7.F89773Hap 2005
[Fic]—dc22   2004031080

In Business with Mallory

For everyone at Lerner—
You make the book business fun!
All my thanks,
—L .B .F.

For my daughter Miranda,
Future businesswoman
—B. P.

In Business with Mallory

by Laurie Friedman
illustrations by Barbara Pollak

MINNEAPOLIS

CONTENTS

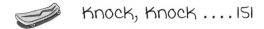

A WORD FROM MALLORY

Have you ever wanted to buy something, but when you ask your parents, they say, "No"? So you say, "Pretty please, with sugar and cream on top!"

Then your parents say, "No! We are not buying that thing."

So you say, "Please, please, please buy that thing! I have to have that thing!" And just in case your parents don't get how important that thing is to you, you hug them and tell them you love them. Then you wait.

You wait for your parents to say, "Awww (fill in your name here), that is the sweetest thing we've ever heard. Of course we'll buy that (fill in the name of the thing you've been talking to them about here) for you."

But that's not what they say.

What they say is, "(put your name here and say it in a not-so-nice way), we will not buy that (say the name of the thing here like you're talking about a bad virus that's going around your school) for you."

And then they say they're through talking and no matter what you say, you're not getting what you want.

And that's when you get a feeling . . . an If-I'm-ever-going-to-get-what-I-want-I'm-going-to-have-to-find-a-way-to-get-it-myself feeling.

If that's something you've felt, then you and I have a lot in common. I'm Mallory McDonald, age just-turned nine, and that's exactly how I'm feeling.

The problem is . . . figuring out what to do about it.

THE PERFECT PURSE

"Max, out of the way! You're blocking *Fashion Fran!*"

I pick up my cat, Cheeseburger, and move from one end of the couch to the other. I want to see my favorite TV show, NOT my brother's back.

Max plops down on the couch where I was sitting. He picks up the remote and starts flipping through the channels.

"Hey! What are you doing?" I try to grab the remote out of his hands, but Max is too fast. He finds a baseball game and then shoves the remote under his seat cushion.

"Who wants to watch a dumb show about what to wear?"

"I do!"

I know Max is going to say, "*Too bad. I don't!*" But I don't wait for him to say it.

"MOM!" I yell. "I was watching *Fashion Fran* and Max changed the channel."

Mom walks into the family room. "Max, take turns. Let Mallory finish her show, then you can pick something you want to watch."

"She can watch whatever she wants," Max says like he was never planning to not let me watch my show. "I'm going outside."

I hate when Max acts like he wasn't doing something that he knows he was doing. I pick up the remote and switch back to Fran.

"Now, for the latest in rain gear," says Fran.

Just as Fran starts modeling a raincoat with matching boots and an umbrella, the phone rings. I pick up the receiver on the coffee table next to the couch before anybody else has a chance to. "Hey, hey, hey!" I say into the phone.

I wait for my lifelong best friend to say *hey, hey, hey* back, but it's not Mary Ann's voice on the other end.

"Hey Mal," says a boy's voice. "Want to meet me at the wish pond and we can go skateboarding?"

I love skateboarding with Joey. Ever since I moved to Wish Pond Road, he's been

a great next-door neighbor, a great skateboarding instructor, and a great friend, but I can't go skateboarding in the middle of my favorite show. "Another day," I tell Joey.

I hang up the phone. While Fran demonstrates how the raincoat can be worn on either side, the phone rings again. "What now?" I ask when I pick up the phone.

But this time, it isn't a boy's voice like I thought it would be.

"Hey, hey, hey!" says a voice on the other end. I grin into the receiver. It's Mary Ann! "Are you watching our favorite show?" she asks me.

Mary Ann and I made a pinkie swear a long time ago to never miss an episode of *Fashion Fran*. "What else would I be doing?" I ask.

Even though it was more fun watching *Fashion Fran* with Mary Ann before I moved to Fern Falls, we still like watching it together. I snuggle into the couch and hold the phone with one hand and Cheeseburger with the other.

Fashion Fran puts away her umbrella. "I'm saving this for a rainy day!" she says with a smile. Then she takes out a shiny purple box. "The next item I have to show you is very special." She opens the lid to the box and pulls out a purse.

"This is not just any purse," says Fashion Fran. "This is the Perfect Purse." She holds the purse up so it fills the TV screen.

"Cute, cute, cute!" gasps Mary Ann.

"So, so, so!" I gasp back. Mary Ann and I always like the same things.

Fran starts taking things out of the purple box.

"The Perfect Purse is perfect because it's not just *one* purse. The Perfect Purse comes with ten custom-designed covers in a variety of today's most fashionable colors, patterns, and textures, including faux fur, leopard print, crushed velvet, sequins, a patriotic stars and stripes pattern, polka dots, and a lovely rainbow design," she says.

"There's even a waterproof cover for rainy days." Fran holds covers up to the TV screen so we can see them at home.

"I love the leopard print," says Mary Ann.

"So do I." The leopard print is definitely my favorite.

"But that's not all," Fashion Fran tells us. "The Perfect Purse also comes with a sparkly butterfly pin to dress up your purse for the most formal of affairs."

The TV shows a picture of Fran in a long red dress. She's carrying the Perfect Purse with the stars and stripes cover on it and the butterfly pinned to it.

"That was me at the Firecracker Ball on the 4th of July," Fran says, smiling.

"Wow," says Mary Ann. "Fran looked so pretty."

"You'll never need another purse if you have

the Perfect Purse," says Fran. She hugs hers to her chest. "Get yours while supplies last. They won't be around for long."

Fashion Fran waves. "That's it for today," she says. "See you tomorrow with more of the latest, greatest finds in the world of fashion." Fran blows a kiss.

I click off the TV. "What a great episode," I say.

"What a great purse," says Mary Ann. "I wish I had one."

"Yeah, me too."

Mary Ann sighs like it's really sad that we don't. Then she squeals into the phone. "Let's both get one! We'll have matching purses!"

I feel like a marching band just marched into my ear. "How are we going to do that?" I ask.

"Simple," says Mary Ann. "I'll ask my

mom to get me one. You ask your mom to get you one."

Mary Ann knows my mom well enough to know that she says *no* to a lot of things. "But what if my mom says *no*?"

"She won't say *no*," says Mary Ann. "Just tell her how perfect the Perfect Purse is and I know she'll get it for you."

I hope Mary Ann is right. I hope Mom will say yes.

"I can't believe I didn't think of this before," Mary Ann says in her marching band voice. "When my mom and I come to visit in two weeks, we can wear our matching purses. It will be fun, fun, fun!"

Mary Ann and her mom come to visit a lot now . . . now that her mom is dating Joey's dad. Even though I'm not sure I like that my old best friend's mom is dating my new best friend's dad, I do like that Mary

Ann comes to Fern Falls more often.

"It sounds like fun," I tell Mary Ann.

"And it will be. You get your mom to get you one. I'll get my mom to get me one. Having the Perfect Purse is all I can think about!" she says.

"Yeah," I tell Mary Ann. But when I hang up the phone, *having* the Perfect Purse isn't all I can think about. *Getting* the Perfect Purse is all I can think about.

I hope it will be as simple as Mary Ann says it will be.

MALL MADNESS

Mom pulls into a parking space at the mall. Our van looks like one tiny goldfish in a big aquarium filled with hundreds of goldfish. There are cars everywhere.

"I think everyone in Fern Falls decided to go shopping today," I say to Mom as we walk toward the mall.

Mom points to a sign hanging over the opening of the mall. "It's Mall Madness."

"Why would anybody get mad about

coming to the mall?" I ask.

Mom laughs as we walk into a department store. "This kind of madness doesn't mean people are angry. It means they're excited. There are a lot of sales going on, so people are excited to go shopping," she explains as we head up the escalator to the Girls' Department.

That makes sense to me. I hadn't thought of it before, but I'm mad too. Mad with excitement, but not to buy the underwear we came to buy. I'm excited to buy what I want, and what I want is the Perfect Purse.

I hope I can find what I'm looking for.

When we get to the Girls' Department, Mom starts looking through a pile of underwear. She holds up a pair in front of her for me to see.

But what I see behind Mom is much more

exciting than what's in front of her. It's the Perfect Purse! I didn't think something so perfect could be so easy to find.

I reach around Mom and pick up a purse off of the display. "It's the Perfect Purse!" I say, holding up the purse for Mom to see.

Mom laughs. "I'm sure it is the perfect purse, but these are the perfect underwear. Your size and on sale." Mom picks up a pink pair and a yellow pair.

I don't know how Mom can think about something as boring as underwear at a time like this.

"Mo-o-o-o-o-o-o-o-o-m! This *really* is the Perfect Purse." I hold it up so she can see what I already know. "Just look! This purse comes with ten covers." I show her the covers on the display. Then I read her the advertisement that is on the back of the box.

"The Perfect Purse comes with ten custom-designed covers in a variety of today's most fashionable colors, patterns, and textures, including faux fur, leopard print, crushed velvet, sequins, a patriotic stars and stripes pattern, polka dots, and a lovely rainbow design. There's even a waterproof cover for rainy days, and a sparkly butterfly pin to dress up your Perfect Purse for the most formal of affairs."

I start to read Mom the part of the ad that says if you buy the Perfect Purse you will never need another purse. But Mom stops me.

"Mallory, we came to buy underwear for you and cleats for Max, not a purse."

I give Mom an *I-want-the-purse-and-not-the-underwear* look. "Mary Ann and I made a promise. She promised her mom would get her one, and I promised you would get me one." I lay the purse gently in Mom's arms, like it's a baby kitten.

Mom looks at the purse in her arms, but not like it's a helpless little animal.

"Mallory, just because Mary Ann is getting it doesn't mean you're going to." Mom looks down at the price tag. "This is a very expensive purse." She pushes the price tag toward me so I can see too.

But I don't need to look to know that it

costs more than most purses. "It costs more than one purse," I tell Mom, "because it's like having ten purses."

Mom looks at me like that doesn't make any sense.

Even though math isn't my best subject, I try to explain. "If we bought ten purses, they would cost more than one purse, so we are actually saving money if we buy the Perfect Purse because it costs less than ten purses."

I wait for my explanation to sink in, but Mom shakes her head. She puts the purse back on the display, picks up an armload of underwear, and walks to the cash register.

I look at the Perfect Purse that Mom put back, and I think about Mary Ann. I bet right now she's at the mall with her mom, and I bet her mom's not buying underwear.

"C'mon, Mallory." Mom says my name in

a *follow-me-and-don't-ask-for-anything-else* look. We go back down the escalator and through the mall.

As we pass the fountain in the courtyard of the mall, I watch the shopping bag in Mom's hand swing back and forth. I can't help wishing that bag was filled with something besides underwear. I tap Mom on the shoulder. "May I please have a penny?"

Mom smiles and opens her purse. "I don't see why not." She hands me a penny.

I squeeze it in my hand and pretend like I'm at the wish pond at the end of my street. I do what I always do when I want something to happen. I make a wish.

I wish somehow, some way, I will get the Perfect Purse.

I throw my penny into the fountain and watch it sink to the bottom. I hope my wish

comes true. I follow Mom to the athletic store to get a pair of cleats for Max.

I'm quiet while Mom shops for Max. When she finishes, we walk back through the department store to go to our car. As we pass the escalator that leads up to the Girls' Department, I put my hand on Mom's arm to stop her.

I think about the penny I threw into the fountain. I think now is the time for my wish to come true.

"Mom." I try to keep my voice calm and talk to her the way grown-ups do when they really want other grown-ups to do something. "I know you already said *no*, but it would make me really happy if you would please buy the Perfect Purse for me."

I try to keep a pleasant look on my face while I wait for Mom's answer.

But I don't have to wait long. I look at

Mom's face, and it doesn't look nearly as pleasant as mine. Her voice doesn't sound calm either.

"Mallory, we are through talking about the Perfect Purse. I said *no,* and I mean *no.*" Mom pulls me by my arm out the door and through the parking lot.

I think about my wish. I guess mall fountains don't work nearly as well as wish ponds. As we head toward our car, I look over my shoulder at the Mall Madness sign.

I have mall madness. But it's definitely not the excited kind.

A PARENT
CONFERENCE

"For you." I walk into the kitchen and hand my parents an envelope.

Mom puts the envelope down on the counter and hands me the phone.

Most days, I love phone calls. But not today. Today, I have something important that I need to do. "Hello," I say in my *I'm-not-in-the-mood-to-talk* voice.

"Hey!" says Joey. "Want to meet by the wish pond in five minutes? If you bring Cheeseburger, I can try to teach her to dance on her back legs. I saw someone teaching a cat to dance on TV and I . . . "

But I don't let Joey finish. "Maybe later," I tell him. Right now, I don't have time to teach my cat to dance.

I pick up the envelope off of the counter. "You need to open this," I say to Mom.

Mom smiles as she takes it from me, but she stops smiling when she sees what's written on the outside. "A Parent Conference," she says out loud.

"I wonder why Mrs. Daily wants to see us?" Dad says.

Mom opens the envelope, and when she reads the note inside, she starts smiling again. "Mrs. Daily doesn't want to see us," Mom says. "Mallory does."

"It's conference time," I tell my parents. I pull two chairs together so my parents can sit down. I talk to them like I'm a teacher. "We need to talk about Mallory."

"Is she OK?" asks Dad. He looks like he's trying not to laugh.

I give Dad a *this-is-serious* look. "Mallory is OK, but she could be doing better."

"Really?" asks Mom. "How could she be doing better?"

I give my parents an encouraging look.

"I wasn't going to tell you this, but since you asked . . ." I stop talking. I feel like I've got an extra-large peanut butter and marshmallow sandwich stuck in my throat.

Telling parents how their child could be doing better isn't as easy as I thought. Especially if you're about to tell them something they might not want to hear.

Dad looks at his watch. "Sweet Potato, I

have to get to work. The store opens early on Saturdays. Can you tell us quickly what the problem is?"

I clear my throat. "It's complicated."

"Let's un-complicate it," he says. "I'll start a sentence, and you fill in the blank."

I nod my head. "OK."

"Here goes," says Dad. "I invited my parents to a conference to tell them I could be doing better if . . . Now, you fill in the rest of the sentence."

Even though it's not easy, I finish Dad's sentence.

"I invited my parents to a conference to tell them I could be doing better if they would buy me the Perfect Purse."

"Mallory, we've discussed this!" says Mom. "That purse is expensive and unnecessary. I can't think of one good reason to buy it."

"I can," I tell Mom. "I can think of ten *very* good reasons to buy the Perfect Purse."

Before Mom or Dad can say anything else, I start reading.

10 Reasons Why I, Mallory McDonald, Need to Buy the Perfect Purse:

#1: The Perfect Purse is stylish. It comes with 10 designer covers.

#2: The Perfect Purse is special. It comes with a sparkly pin.

#3: The Perfect Purse is versatile. You can use it as a purse, a ~~tote~~, or a carryall.

#4: The Perfect Purse is practical. It has a waterproof cover for rainy days.

#5: The Perfect Purse is economical. You will never have to buy another purse.

#6: The Perfect Purse is exclusive. Limited quantities are available.

#7: The Perfect Purse is chic. Fashionable girls everywhere are carrying it.

#8: I will love having the Perfect Purse. It will be like having a new best friend.

#9: Mary Ann is getting the Perfect Purse. I need to get one so we can match.

#10: If I get the Perfect Purse, I will be perfectly happy. My happiness will make me a better daughter, a better sister, and a better student too.

"Mallory, you sound like a commercial," Dad says when I finish reading.

"Even worse than sounding like a commercial," says Mom, "is that you sound spoiled. Just because Mary Ann is getting one, doesn't mean that you can too."

"But I *need* to get one. Mary Ann and I are planning to get matching purses. Please," I say to my parents.

"You and Mary Ann don't always get the same things," Mom says. "She didn't get a cat when you got Cheeseburger."

I don't know how we got on the subject of cats when we are supposed to be talking about purses. "I didn't get a cat," I remind Mom. "I found her."

"Everyone gets different things," says Dad. "And you're not getting the purse."

"Will you at least think about it?" I ask. But both of my parents shake their heads *no* at the same time. "Mallory, this is the last time we're going to discuss this," says Mom.

Mom stands up. "Conference time is over." She puts her chair back at the table.

Dad puts his chair back too. He kisses me on the forehead. "I'm going to work."

After Dad leaves, I go into the family room and plop down on the couch with Cheeseburger. Max and his dog, Champ, are watching a show I don't even like. But I

don't care.   All I can think about is my parent conference.

My conference didn't go well. If parents got graded on conference behavior, my parents would get a "U" for uncooperative.

When I hear the mail truck, I run outside to see if I got anything. The postman hands me a stack of letters. Joey is playing in his front yard. He waves to me.

I wave back, then I look through the mail to see if there's anything for me, and there is . . . a letter from Mary Ann! I sit down in front of the mailbox and rip it open.

Dear Mallory,

Good news! My mom bought me the Perfect Purse!

I can't wait till I wear mine!

I can't wait till you wear yours!

I can't wait till we match! See you soon, and when I do, everything will be perfect, perfect, perfect . . . especially our purses!

Love,

Mary Ann

When I'm done reading, I lean back against the mailbox. I can feel the cold steel of the pole through my sweater. Mary Ann is wrong about one thing. Everything will not be perfect, perfect, perfect . . . not if I don't have the Perfect Purse too.

While I'm busy imagining Mary Ann with

her purse, and me without mine, Joey walks over to our front porch. "Want me to teach Cheeseburger some tricks now?"

I shake my head *no*.

"Feel like skateboarding?"

I shake my head *no* again.

"We could just go down to the wish pond and skip rocks."

I shake my head *no* a third time. "I don't feel like it."

Joey makes a mad face. "You never feel like playing anymore."

"I'm sorry," I tell Joey. I don't want him to think I don't want to be his friend.

I try to explain about the Perfect Purse.

When I'm done explaining, I look at Joey. He always understands things. But this time, he doesn't look like he understands at all.

"Mallory, who cares about a dumb old purse?"

Even though I can see Joey doesn't care, I do, and I know someone else who might care too. "We can play some other time," I tell Joey.

I scoop up Cheeseburger. "Right now, I have to make a phone call."

A PHONE CALL

I tiptoe up the stairs into Mom and Dad's room. I put Cheeseburger down on a chair and close the door. I pick up the receiver and punch the buttons on the keypad.

When the phone starts ringing, I cross my toes. I hope the person I'm calling is home because I really need to talk to her.

The phone rings. Once. Twice. Three times. Finally a voice answers.

"Hello."

"Grandma!" I scream. "Surprise! It's me, Mallory!"

"What a wonderful surprise!" says Grandma. "How's my little Honey Bee?"

"Not so good," I tell her.

"Oh no!" says Grandma like she can't think of anything worse than me not feeling good. "Do you want to tell me what's the matter? Maybe I can help."

"I hope you can help me, because Mom and Dad haven't been any help at all."

"I'm all ears," says Grandma.

I giggle. I know Grandma means she's listening to every word I'm saying, but I can't help imagining what Grandma would look like if she were all ears.

"Here's the problem. There's this purse called the Perfect Purse . . ." And before I can stop myself, I start telling Grandma everything about the Perfect Purse.

"It's the latest and the greatest and it comes with ten covers and a sparkly pin and Mary Ann is getting one and I want one so we can match and . . ."

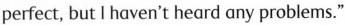

"Whoa!" Grandma laughs. "Slow down. So far I've heard lots of reasons why the purse is perfect, but I haven't heard any problems."

"There is a problem," I tell Grandma in my *there's-only-one-problem-but-it's-a-big-one* voice. "Mom and Dad won't get it for me.

"And that's where I come in?" asks Grandma.

"Exactly!" I say.

"Well," says Grandma. "You've come to the right person. I think I can help you."

I knew Grandma would understand. "So you'll get the Perfect Purse for me?"

Grandma laughs again. "Honey Bee, I'm going to help you get the Perfect Purse."

"What do you mean?" I ask, even though I'm not sure I really want to know.

Grandma sighs into the phone. "Mallory, I'm going to tell you a story."

I sit back on the bed. Now I think it's my turn to be all ears.

"When I was a young girl, there was a doll I wanted," says Grandma. "She had glass eyes and real hair and her clothes were made of the finest silk. One day I tore a picture of the doll out of a magazine and showed it to my parents."

"Did they get it for you?" I ask.

"No, they didn't get it for me, even though I begged and pleaded and promised I would do anything if they would just get me the doll."

Grandma's parents sound a lot like mine.

Grandma continues her story. "My parents told me the doll was very expensive, and that even though she was beautiful, they thought she was a silly waste of money."

"So what did you do?"

"I decided to buy the doll myself."

Grandma must have gotten a lot of birthday money that year. "So you had enough to pay for the doll yourself?"

"Not exactly. I had to go to work to make enough money to buy the doll."

"But you were just a kid," I remind Grandma. "Wasn't

it hard to make money?"

"It was indeed," says Grandma. "But I started a business going door to door selling oranges for a penny until I had enough to buy the doll."

I think about how much the Perfect Purse costs. "I think I'll have to sell a lot of oranges to buy what I want."

"Maybe you want to do something other than sell oranges."

"Like what?" I ask Grandma.

"Give it some thought," says Grandma. "Talk to some people. I'm sure you'll come up with something."

The only thing I wanted to be thinking about after this phone call was carrying a purse, not starting a business.

"Good luck, Honey Bee, and let me know what happens." Grandma blows me kisses over the phone before she hangs up.

I pick up Cheeseburger and walk back downstairs to my room. Maybe Grandma is right. Maybe that is what I need to do.

Once, I saw a TV interview of Fashion Fran. She started her first business selling hand-painted T-shirts. She said she couldn't believe how many people bought her T-shirts. Maybe I should sell something too.

I take Cheeseburger into my closet to look for things to sell. I see lots of things, but no things I want to sell.

I sit down at my desk and take out a sheet of paper. I write *Things I Can Sell* on the top of the paper. I try to write a list of things I can sell, but the only thing I can think about is writing a letter.

I take out a fresh sheet of paper and begin.

Dear Mary Ann,
This is a letter, but it's not a regular letter. It's a business letter.
(A business letter is a letter you write when you're going into business, and that's exactly what I'm planning to do.)
I bet you have a lot of questions like: Why am I going into business and what

kind of business am I going into? Well, here are some answers.

I am going into business because I have to . . . if I want to get the Perfect Purse.

And I don't have any idea what kind of business I'm going into. But I do know this: I'm going to sell something that a lot of people will want to buy so I can get the Perfect Purse and we can match when you come to visit.

I think that sounds like a good plan, don't you?

Well, that's all for now. I've got to go start my business. You will be here soon, soon, soon. And when you get here, I want to make sure I have the Perfect

Purse too.

(So don't worry, by the time you get here, we will match, match, match.)

Yours truly (I think that's how you end a business letter),

mallory

When I'm done writing, I stick my business letter in an envelope. Now all I have to do is go start a business. How hard can it be?

WHAT A JOKE!

When I walk into the kitchen, Mom and Max are sitting at the table. Mom smiles at me. "Max and I are putting together a list of who he wants to invite to his birthday dinner."

"Yeah," says Max, "so make like a tree and leave."

Mom gives Max an *if-you-can't-say-something-nice-don't-say-anything* look.

I almost forgot my brother is turning

eleven in two weeks. I hope when he does, he starts acting his age. "I don't want to interrupt, but I need a box."

"Are you moving?" asks Max. "If you are, I'll help you pack."

I ignore Max. I know he isn't really trying to be helpful. "I'm not moving. I'm starting a business selling joke books. I need a box for my books," I tell Mom.

Max laughs. "You're starting a joke book selling business?" Max laughs even harder. "What a joke!"

Mom puts down her pencil. "Honey, why would you sell your joke books?"

I love my joke books. Grandma gave me my first one when I learned to read. I've been collecting them ever since.

But here's the thing: I think other people will love them too.

"I'm selling them because I need

money," I tell Mom.

Mom frowns. "Mallory, what do you need money for?"

I scratch my head and do some fast thinking. I know Mom won't like hearing that I need money to buy the Perfect Purse, but there's something else I think Mom *will* like hearing. I look at Max. "I need money to buy Max's birthday present."

The frown on Mom's face turns into a smile. "That is very sweet," she says. "But you don't have to sell your joke books to buy a present for your brother."

I look at Max. "I want to."

Max smiles like he likes the idea that I'm willing to sell my joke books to buy him a birthday present, but that he can't believe that I am.

I smile back. With *part* of the money, I am going to buy him a present. And with the other part, I'm going to buy what I want.

I pull a square of paper out of my pocket and hand it to Mom. "Here's my card."

Mom reads from the card. "Joke books for sale. Contact Mallory McDonald at 17 Wish Pond Road. Ha ha! Tee hee!" Mom smiles, then she gets a serious look on her face. "Mallory, who are you planning to sell your joke books to?"

I knew Mom would ask me that question, and I've already thought of an answer.

"I'm going to go next door to the Winstons'. I'll ask Mrs. Black down the street. I'll ask the other neighbors. I'll call Pamela. And I'll ask my other friends at school. I'll sell a joke book to anybody that wants to buy one."

Mom puts her arm around me. "It's hard work finding something that people want to buy."

"Good luck," says Max. But I can tell by looking at him that he's not so sure my plan is going to work. But I think it's going to.

I think of Grandma and her oranges. I'd rather buy a joke book than a piece of fruit. "All I can do is try," I tell Mom.

Mom pats me on the head. "There's a box in the laundry room you can use."

I get the box and take it into my room. I fill it with joke books and write *Joke Books* on the side of the box.

Then I walk down to the wish pond with my box and make a wish. *I wish I sell a lot of joke books.* Mary Ann will be here next weekend, and I want to have my purse when she gets here.

I walk to the Winstons' and ring the bell. When Winnie answers the door, she looks at my box. "What do you want?" she asks.

I feel like a Girl Scout selling cookies. "Want to buy a joke book?"

Winnie snorts. "Get a life. I'll go get Joey."

I wish joke books came in yummy flavors like thin mint or peanut butter sandwich. If they did, they'd be easier to sell.

When Joey comes to the door, I explain what I'm selling.

Joey looks through my box. "I love joke books. But I'm saving my money to buy a new skateboard."

He points down the street. "Why don't you try Mrs. Black. She buys everything."

I walk to Mrs. Black's house and ring the doorbell. "I'm selling joke books," I tell her

when she opens the door. "Would you like to buy one?"

Mrs. Black frowns. "I like candy, cookies, and wrapping paper. But I'm afraid I'm the wrong person for a joke book. Perhaps you'll have better luck at another house."

But I don't have luck at any other houses, even though I go to every single one of them on my street. No one wants to buy a joke book.

I walk home with my box. Even though I didn't add any books to it, it feels heavier than it did before.

When I get home, I go into the kitchen and call Pamela. I hope she will be my first customer.

"Hi Pamela, want to buy a joke book?" I ask in my cheeriest voice when she answers. I tell her all about the different joke books I'm selling.

"Hold on," says Pamela. "Let me ask my mom."

I cross my toes while I wait. I hope Pamela's mom says yes.

But she doesn't. "Sorry," says Pamela. "I can't buy a joke book."

"That's OK," I mumble into the phone. I tell Pamela good-bye and carry my box of books to my room and drop it on the floor. I sit down on the box and pull Cheeseburger into my lap. "No one wanted to buy a joke book," I tell her.

Max sticks his head into my room. "No luck, huh?"

I can't believe Max was listening to my private conversation with my cat. I'm sure he's going to remind me that selling joke books was a big joke.

"OUT!" I say to my brother.

But Max doesn't go out. He comes into

my room and sits down on my floor.

"I'm just trying to help," he says. "Think about it from my perspective. If you don't sell something soon, I'm not getting much of a birthday present. Let me give you a little advice," says Max. "If at first you don't succeed, try again."

"Thanks a lot," I mumble. The only thing I'd like to succeed at is selling my brother.

A BUSINESS FLOP

Dear Mary Ann,

I am a business flop.

If you don't know what that means, I'll tell you.

It means I stink at business! That's right. I tried four businesses in four days and each one was a big, fat failure. Keep reading and you will see what I mean.

BUSINESS FLOP #1:
JOKE BOOKS SELLING BUSINESS
    I tried selling my joke books.
    I tried to sell them to my friends. I tried to sell them to my neighbors. I tried to sell them to anyone that I thought might buy one. And guess what . . . NO ONE did.
    I didn't sell one joke books.
    This business was a big flop.

BUSINESS FLOP #2:
GIRL FOR HIRE
    I gried to work for people.
    I told people that I would do anything they wanted me to do, and all they had to do was pay me. At first, this seemed

like a good idea.

I worked for Mom. I made her lunch She paid me a quarter.

I worked for Dad. I swept the garage. He paid me fifty cents.

I worked for Max. I cleaned his room. He paid me a dime.

I worked for Joey. I put his socks into pairs. He paid me a nickel.

I worked for Winnie. I folded her clothes. She paid me another nickel.

I worked all day and all I made was ninety-five cents!

That is not a lot of money to make for a hard day's work.

This business was an even bigger flop.

BUSINESS FLOP#3:
SKATEBOARDING DEMONSTRATIONS

I thought this was my best business idea ever. I wanted Joey to do skateboarding demonstrations. People would pay to see him and he would pay me for coming up with this great idea.

Here's the good news:

Joey wanted to do it and people wanted to pay to see him do it.

Here's the bad news:

Joey didn't want to pay me for coming up with the idea. He said he'd been thinking about doing skateboarding demonstrations for a long time, and that even though I'm his good friend, he didn't know why he should pay me if he had to do all the work.

Are you starting to see what I mean about me being a business flop?

BUSINESS FLOP #4:
COMIC STRIP STAND

You're probably thinking it is impossible for another business to flop, but trust me, this business was the biggest flop of all.

I decided to sell cartoons. I set up a stand in the foront yard. I got out all my paper and pencils. I was ready to draw.

But nobody came to get a comic. Nobody.

Well, actually mom came. I drew one comic strip for her (see end of this letter), but she said she wouldn't buy it because it was too negative. So I didn't sell any comic strips.

See, I told you I AM A BIG, FAT BUSIENSS FLOP. And if you ask me, being a business flop is almost as bad as doing a bellyflop.

Now I can't buy the Perfect Purse, so we can't have matching purses.

I thought I would have fun being in business. I thought I would make a lot of money. I thought I would be able to buy whatever I wanted. But I think when it comes to business, all I have are dumb ideas.

I wish there was some kind of business where I could have fun and make a lot of money. Like a salon. Wouldn't that be fun? We could do it together.

We could do hair and nails and makeup. We could give out little cookies with m's on top. And we could wear matching T-shirts.

maybe that's what we'll do when we grow up. maybe then I can buy the Perfect Purse. (Do you think they will run out of them before we are grown-ups?)

I hope this letter did not make you too sad.

It makes me sad.

my tears are about to fall out on this page,

mallory

P.S. Here is the comic strip I drew for mom. (And don't worry, you don't have to pay me for it.)

TALE OF A BUSINESS FLOP

written and illustrated by Mallory McDonald

MARY ANN TO THE RESCUE

Dear Mallory,

I got your letter.
I'm sorry to hear you think you're a business flop (at least you're not a flip-flop).
You might think your ideas are dumb, but I don't.

I love, love, love your salon idea!!!!!!!!!!!!!!!!!!!

It would be so much fun to have our own salon.

Everything would be just like you said it would be.

Hey, maybe we don't have to wait until we grow up. (Don't forget, we won't be grown-ups for a long time.) Maybe we can have a salon now. (Not right now, but this weekend when I come to visit.)

Wouldn't that be fun, fun, fun?!?

What do you think?

See you in a few days.

Can't wait, wait, wait!

Hugs and kisses,
Mary Ann

I fold Mary Ann's letter and put it on my desk.

"Maybe Mary Ann is right," I say to Cheeseburger.

Maybe we don't have to wait until we're grown-ups to have a salon. Maybe Mary Ann and I *can* have a salon when she comes to town this weekend with her mom.

The more I think about it, the more I love, love, love the idea.

SALON MALLORY

Ding-dong.

"I'll get it!" Mary Ann and I yell at the same time. We run down the hall to open the front door. But before we do, we do one final check.

T-shirts. Check. We're wearing the matching *Salon Mallory* T-shirts we made.

Hair. Check. We pinned up our hair with

coordinating hair clips.

Nails. Check. We painted our fingernails ten different colors.

Since the moment Mary Ann arrived in Fern Falls, we've been working hard to

make sure *Salon Mallory* is a big success.

Last night, we called my friends in my class to remind them about their salon appointments. We set up hair, nail, and makeup stations in my room. We even made a big sign that says *Salon Mallory* to hang on the door of my room.

This morning, we're ready for business. Mary Ann and I look at each other and nod. "Welcome to *Salon Mallory!*" we say as we fling the front door open.

Pamela, April, Danielle, Arielle, Brittany, Dawn, Emma, and Grace are there, and so is Jackson.

Mary Ann giggles. "We didn't expect any boys," she whispers to me.

"Jackson, what are you doing here?" I ask.

He takes a notebook and pencil out of his pocket. "When Mrs. Daily heard about the salon, she said I should come write an article about it for *The Daily News*."

"Wow!" says Mary Ann. "We're going to be famous!"

"*The Daily News* is the school newspaper that our classroom writes," I explain to my best friend.

"Who cares which newspaper we're going to be in," shrieks Mary Ann. "We're going to be in a newspaper! Follow me," she says to all my friends.

Everyone walks down the hall behind Mary Ann.

As we walk toward my room, I make a wish in my head. *I wish this business won't flop like my other businesses.*

When we get to my room, I start on hair, and Mary Ann does makeup.

"Over here." I point Pamela to the hair station. I brush and braid her hair.

"Can you tie a ribbon in it?" asks Pamela.

I give Pamela a big box of ribbons to choose from. She picks a yellow one, and I tie it onto the bottom of her braid.

Mary Ann leads Danielle and Arielle over to the makeup table. "You can pick whatever color eye shadow you like."

"I want violet." Danielle points to a shimmery, light purple.

"Me too," says Arielle.

Mary Ann dabs matching shadow on both of their lids.

While I'm combing out Brittany's hair, and Mary Ann is brushing lip gloss on Emma, Max sticks his head in my room. "What's going on in here?" he asks.

Mary Ann stops brushing. "We're trying to earn money so Mallory can buy . . ."

But I cough before Mary Ann can say *the Perfect Purse*. And I keep coughing. Max doesn't need to know that I'm planning to buy a present AND a purse.

Mary Ann goes back to brushing lip gloss on Emma. "I don't see your name on the appointment book," she says to Max. "No need to stick around, unless you want your hair or makeup done."

Usually, Max would say something

obnoxious to Mary Ann, but he surprises me. He just gives me an *I-think-salons-are-stupid-but-if-that's-what-you-have-to-do-to-buy-me-a-birthday-present-then-it's-okay-with-me* look.

Max walks out. I go back to combing and braiding. Mary Ann keeps brushing

and dabbing. We don't stop all morning.

Jackson sits at my desk taking notes. Then he takes out a camera. "I need a picture to go with the article." He takes a few shots while we work.

"Wow!" says Emma when she sees her makeup. "I look like I'm eleven." Everyone looks in my mirror . . . and everyone looks like they're happy.

When we finish with hair and makeup, Mary Ann and I start on nails.

"We have ten different colors of polishes, and you can choose whatever combination you like," I tell my friends.

Our customers start looking through the bottles of polish at the nail station.

"I want light yellow," Pamela says.

April wants green with blue dots.

Danielle and Arielle choose purple to match their eye shadow.

Brittany, Dawn, Emma, and Grace want the same thing Mary Ann and I have . . . ten fingers, ten colors.

While everyone is letting their nails dry, Mom comes into my room with the platter of cookies with M's on top and the lemonade Mary Ann and I made last night.

"Those cookies are so cute!" says Grace.

Mom puts the platter down. She smiles like she approves of the results at *Salon Mallory*. "Be careful," says Mom. "You don't want to mess up your nails."

Everyone eats cookies and drinks lemonade like they're fancy ladies at a tea party. When they're through, they pay us and get ready to leave.

"Thanks for coming to *Salon Mallory!*" Mary Ann and I wave good-bye.

"Phew!" Mary Ann collapses on my bed after everyone is gone. "That was a lot of work." She takes a deep breath like all that brushing and painting made her tired.

I'm tired too, but not too tired to count what we earned this morning. I start to make neat stacks of all the coins, but Mary Ann pushes them into one big pile. "You don't need to count it," she says. "Just look how much is there."

I eye the money on my floor. Mary Ann

is right. There is a lot. "I'm going to have to wear pants with big pockets to take all that to the mall tomorrow," I say.

Mary Ann giggles. We start pushing money through the little slot on the tip of my piggy bank. While we're pushing, Joey knocks on my window. I get up and open it. "Want to come outside and play?" he asks Mary Ann and me.

"Maybe later," says Mary Ann before I even have time to answer.

Joey nods at Mary Ann like it's no problem, but then he looks at me like it is a problem. I can tell Joey is upset.

I start to say *sorry,* but before I do, Joey walks away.

I feel like ever since Mary Ann and I agreed to get matching Perfect Purses, I've been so busy trying to think of how I'm going to get mine, I haven't had time to play with Joey. The problem is, I don't know what to do about it.

If I ever get the Perfect Purse, I'll be glad to have it for two reasons.

One: I can't wait to have it.

Two: I can't wait to be done getting it.

After Joey leaves, Mary Ann and I go back to pushing coins into my piggy bank. When we're done, I pick it up and shake it. It's so full, it barely makes a noise when I shake it. It's heavy too.

I hand it to Mary Ann so she can feel it. "I can't believe how much you have," she says.

"I probably have enough to buy ten Perfect Purses and a birthday present for Max," I tell her. "And I couldn't have done it without you."

"That's what best friends are for." Mary Ann hands me her Perfect Purse. "Here, try this on."

I hold her purse and model it in front of the mirror. "How do I look?"

"Cute, cute, cute!" squeals Mary Ann. "I can't wait to go to the mall tomorrow! We're going to have matching purses! We can wear them to dinner tomorrow night."

Mary Ann jumps around and hugs me. Even though my best friend gets excited about a lot of things, I haven't seen her this excited in a long time.

Seeing her excited makes me excited too. It will be fun having matching purses. I hug Mary Ann back, and then I pick up Cheeseburger and hug her too. I know tomorrow will be the best, best, best day ever.

I can't think of anything that could mess it up.

DECISIONS, DECISIONS

"Mallory, hurry up. You came to the mall to buy a birthday present for your brother." Mom taps her foot like she's getting impatient with me.

I know one of the things I planned to buy was a present for Max. But when I made that plan, I didn't know I'd barely have enough money to buy what I wanted for myself.

Mom was right about one thing . . . the only NOT perfect thing about the Perfect Purse is the price. I can't believe how much it costs!

There's no way I can buy the purse *and* a present. I put the Perfect Purse that I'm holding back on the display.

"C'mon!" Mary Ann picks up the purse and pulls on my sleeve. "We came to get the Perfect Purse, so get it."

Mom puts her hand on my back and pushes me away from the purse display. "Why don't we go look in Sporting Goods? Max might like some baseball cards."

Mary Ann keeps pulling. Mom keeps pushing. I feel like Mom and Mary Ann are playing tug-of-war and the rope that they're pulling on is me.

I don't think Mom understands that

buying a present for Max isn't so simple. I know Max will be a little upset if I don't get him a birthday present, but Mary Ann will be a LOT upset if I don't get the purse.

I wish I didn't have to choose, but that's a wish I know won't come true.

I try to explain things to Mom. "Mary Ann and I worked hard yesterday to make enough money so we can have matching purses. I only have enough to buy the Perfect Purse. I don't have enough to buy the purse *and* a present for Max."

I think I explained things pretty well.

I cross my toes. I hope Mom understands. But she doesn't look like she does. Mom crosses something too, and it's not her toes.

She crosses her arms across her chest. "Mallory, I understand that you want to buy the purse. And I understand that Mary

Ann wants you to have it. But it's your brother's birthday. Don't you think you should get him something?"

"She could make him a card," says Mary Ann.

Sometimes my best friend has the best ideas, and this is one of those times.

"That's a great idea!" I say to Mom. "You know I'm good at making things. I'll make Max a really special card."

But I can tell by the look on Mom's face that she doesn't think making Max a card is nearly as good an idea as Mary Ann and I think it is.

Mom puts her hand on my arm. "Mary Ann, will you excuse us for a minute? Mallory and I need to have a word alone." Mom pulls me over to the other side of the purse display and starts whispering.

"Mallory, you have a decision to make.

You can either buy the Perfect Purse with all of your money or you can buy your brother a birthday present with some of it and have some left over to buy something for yourself."

I start to say something, but Mom holds her finger up, which I know means she's not done talking yet.

"I'm sure you know how I feel about this. We've already talked about the price of the Perfect Purse. There are lots of other, less expensive purses. You're nine years old, and I'm going to let you make your own decision."

Then Mom looks at me in a very serious way. "I'm counting on you to make the right decision." I follow Mom as she walks back toward Mary Ann.

On the one hand, I really want the Perfect Purse. I worked hard to get it, and

so did Mary Ann. I know she will be
disappointed if I don't get it.

On the other hand, I know if I don't
get Max a birthday present, Mom
will be unhappy with me. Max will be
disappointed too.

I know I have to make a decision. The
problem is . . . it's a hard decision to make.
I look at Mom. She looks like she's waiting
for me to make one decision. I look at
Mary Ann. She looks like she's waiting for
me to make another decision.

I think about doing eenie, meenie,
miney, mo to help me decide, but I don't
think that's the answer.

"C'mon!" Mary Ann tugs on me. "What
are you waiting for?"

I try to explain, but the words won't
come out of my mouth.

Mary Ann puts her arm around me and

looks at Mom. "Will you excuse us for a minute?" she says. "Mallory and I need to have a word alone."

Mary Ann steers me away from Mom and starts whispering. "Earth to Mallory," she says in a low voice. "You're talking about Max. Max who is mean to you. Max who is mean to me. Max who doesn't even let you watch your favorite TV show."

Maybe Mary Ann is right. Max can be mean, and he does change the channel whenever *Fashion Fran* is on. "But he is my brother and it is his birthday and he did get me something on my birthday," I tell Mary Ann.

"And you're going to make him a very special card," says Mary Ann.

She steers me back over to the purse display. She picks up a purse and lays it gently in my arms. "C'mon, Mal."

I look down at the Perfect Purse . . . the shiny, beautiful Perfect Purse. Lying there in my arms, it really does look perfect.

Mary Ann is right. I will make Max a card. I will make him a very special card with my best paper and glitter and stickers.

I look up at Mary Ann and even though the corner of my lip barely curls upwards, she knows me well enough to know what

I'm thinking.

Mary Ann throws her arms around me. "We're going to have so much fun having matching purses, and we can start wearing them tonight! You made the right decision," she says smiling.

I sure hope Mary Ann is right. I smile back at her, but I'm scared to even look at Mom. Something tells me she's not smiling.

A BAD NIGHT

"Good night," says Mary Ann. "Sleep tight and don't let the bedbugs bite."

"Good night." I tell Mary Ann to sleep tight and not to let the bedbugs bite too. I hope they don't bite my best friend, but right now, I don't care if they chew me to bits.

Even though Mary Ann and I told each other good night, I think tonight was a bad night. If I had a diary, which I don't, this is what I'd write in it.

Dear Diary,

Tonight I went to the Fondue Pot with my family, the Winstons, and Mary Ann and her mom.

Most Saturday nights, the grown-ups go out and the kids stay home. But tonight, the grown-ups took the kids out to dinner with them.

Mom said it was going to be a special night. But if you ask me, it was an especially bad night.

It didn't start out that way. It started out especially good.

First, Mary Ann and I got dressed alike. We wore matching shirts, skirts, and shoes. And matching purses . . . matching Perfect Purses with polka dot covers. Everybody said we looked cute, cute, cute.

That was the good part of the night. Here's where it all went wrong.

When we got to the restaurant, the waitress brought two fondue pots to the table. One was full of melted cheese and the other one was filled with hot oil.

She gave us these long forks called fondue forks and told us to use them for dipping and cooking.

We dipped pieces of bread in the melted cheese pot. Then we cooked little chunks of chicken and steak in the pot full of hot oil.

I know, you're thinking all that sounds good, and it was. But I haven't gotten to the bad part yet. Here's the bad part.

After dinner, we had chocolate fondue for dessert. The waitress brought a big pot full of melted chocolate to the table. Then she put down a tray of graham crackers, marshmallows, strawberries, and angel food cake. She said we could dip everything in the chocolate for dessert.

I bet you're thinking this sounds like the best part of all, but here's why it wasn't.

Joey stuck his fondue fork in a marshmallow. Then he stuck the marshmallow in the chocolate. When it was all covered in chocolate, he pulled it out. The chocolate covered marshmallow was supposed to go into his mouth, but it didn't.

It fell off his fork and it landed on my Perfect Purse!

Mr. Winston and Mary Ann's mom tried to clean off my purse with their

napkins, but it only made it look worse. Joey said he was sorry, that it was an accident.

Then everybody had something to say:

"You shouldn't have put your purse on the table," said Winnie.

"Who cares about a stupid purse anyway?" said Max.

"The chocolate spot looks like a polka dot," said Dad.

"We can try to wash it when we get home," said Mom.

"You still have nine other covers," said Mary Ann.

She put her arm around me and smiled. But I could tell she was glad Joey didn't spill melted chocolate on her purse.

Everybody kept eating chocolate

fondue, but I felt so awful, I couldn't even enjoy what I know would have been my favorite dessert ever.

In the van on the way home, Mary Ann said she could tell that I was really upset about what happened in the restaurant. Then she said that she is so, so, so glad we got matching Perfect Purses, even if one of my covers has a chocolate stain on it.

She asked me if I was still glad too.

I told her I was. But here's something I didn't tell Mary Ann.

I'm not sure if I am.

So far, owning the Perfect Purse hasn't been as perfect as I thought it would be.

I know Mary Ann loves having hers. I know I really wanted to get mine. But I'm not having as much fun having it as I

thought I would. All you can do is put
stuff in it and take it places, and then it
just gets dirty.
   The end.

   mallory

I pull
Cheeseburger
close to me,
then I close
two things: my
pretend journal
and my eyes.

THE WORST DAY

Usually, I hate getting up for school, but not today.

Today, I pop out of bed and pull on my stretchy velvet pants and striped turtleneck. Then, I snap my leopard print purse cover onto my Perfect Purse. I can't wait to go to school because I'm taking my Perfect Purse with me.

Even though I didn't have fun using my Perfect Purse at dinner, I went to a lot of trouble to get it, so today I'm giving it a second chance.

Today is going to be the best day ever!

When I'm finished snapping, I hold my purse in my hand and look in the mirror. "You look *mah-va-lous dahl-ing*," I say to myself. Actually, I think I look like a movie star. I give Cheeseburger a movie star kiss on each cheek, and then I head down the hall.

"Mallory, we're having eggs," Mom says when I walk into the kitchen.

I peek in the pan. The eggs look squishy and jiggly. I bet movie stars don't eat squishy, jiggly eggs for breakfast.

"I'll just have a granola bar," I tell Mom. I take one from the box in the pantry.

Mom plucks the granola bar out of my hand and puts the plate of eggs in front of me. "Just a few bites," she says.

Even though eating eggs is the last thing I want to do this morning, I take a few bites. Nothing is going to mess up my day today, not even squishy eggs.

When I'm done, I kiss Mom on the cheek. "Got to run," I tell her.

"What's the rush?" she asks.

"I just can't wait to get to school," I tell Mom.

She rumples my hair. "I like seeing you so enthusiastic."

I am enthusiastic. I can't wait to show my Perfect Purse to my friends. I can already hear what they're going to say:

"That purse is so cool!" Pamela will say.

"That purse is so awesome!" Arielle will say.

"What a lovely purse!" Mrs. Daily will say with a big smile.

I stop next door at the Winston's to get Joey. "Notice anything different?" I ask as we walk to school.

Joey looks at me. "You look the same to me as you always look."

Joey must need to have his eyes tested. "Look again," I tell him.

Joey looks up at my head, then down at my feet. "Nothing," he says.

Joey looked at the top and at the bottom. But I don't think he did a good job looking at the middle. I move my Perfect Purse so I'm holding it right in front of my body . . . right where Joey can see it. "Now do you see anything different?" I ask.

Joey shakes his head. "Move the purse and maybe I can tell."

Even though Joey is one of my best

friends, sometimes he acts like such a boy.
I wave my purse in front of his face. "This
is what's different," I tell him. "What do
you think of this cover?"

Joey groans. "Enough with this purse
stuff. That's all you ever talk about
anymore." Joey walks ahead of me until he
gets to Room 310.

When I walk into the classroom, Mrs.
Daily tells everyone to take their seats.

"Let's get started," she says. "Please take out your math books."

I take out my math book and so does my desk mate, Pamela.

"Please turn to page 112," says Mrs. Daily.

Pamela starts turning pages in her book, but I stop her. I lay my Perfect Purse down on top of her math book. "Look!" I whisper to Pamela. "What do you think?"

I wait for Pamela to tell me she thinks my purse is cool, but that's not what she tells me. "Mallory, put that away." Pamela tries to scoot the purse off her side of the desk. "We're going to get in trouble," she whispers.

"Girls," Mrs. Daily looks in our direction, "are you paying attention?"

Pamela looks toward the front of the room at Mrs. Daily's desk and nods like the answer is *yes, we are paying attention*.

Maybe she is, but I don't know how anyone could pay attention to math when there are much more exciting things to pay attention to . . . like a new purse.

I turn around in my seat to Danielle and Arielle's desks. "Look!" I say in my *you-won't-believe-what-I-have* voice. I wave my Perfect Purse in front of their faces. "Do you like my purse?" I wait for them to say it is so *awesome*.

But they don't. Arielle blows out her breath. "That purse is so last year," she whispers.

What? I can't believe what I just heard! Arielle is wrong, wrong, wrong! "This purse is so *not* last year," I start to explain to her.

"Girls! What's going on back there?" Mrs. Daily asks from the front of the classroom.

"Nothing," says Arielle out loud.

"We're in the middle of math," Danielle whispers to me like I'm preventing her from learning something that she really cares about.

But I know Danielle doesn't care all that much about math. "Did you know this purse comes with ten designer covers?" I whisper to her.

I start to tell her about the sparkly butterfly pin, but before I do, someone says my name.

"Mallory!"

I turn around slowly. Mrs. Daily is standing in front of my desk. "What is going on back here?"

"We're trying to pay attention," says Arielle, "but Mallory keeps trying to show us her new purse."

Mrs. Daily looks down at the purse in my hands. I can tell by the way she's looking at it that she doesn't think it is lovely like I thought she would.

Suddenly, my Perfect Purse doesn't feel so perfect.

"Mallory, why don't you give me the purse, and I'll keep it on my desk." She reaches out her hand to take it from me.

I feel like Dorothy in *The Wizard of Oz* when the Wicked Witch tries to take her ruby slippers.

I clutch my purse to me to keep it safe, but Mrs. Daily pulls it out of my hands. "I'll keep it until the end of the day. You can have it when school is over," she says.

I look down at my empty hands.

When I woke up this morning, I thought today would be the best day ever. I should have known it wouldn't be when I had to eat squishy eggs.

HAPPY BIRTHDAY, MAX!

Question: What has red hair, a sombrero on his head, and is 11 years old today?

Answer: My brother, Max.

We're at Max's favorite restaurant, Casa Taco, and he's with his favorite friends: Adam, Ben, Jared, Dylan, Brett, and Myles.

Actually, I like Casa Taco too. It's one of the few things Max and I agree on.

"Happy Birthday, Max!" Adam jumps on my brother. He takes the sombrero off of Max's head, messes up his hair, and then shoves the hat back on his head.

Max gives Adam a birthday high five.

I jump out of Adam's way. I don't want him to mess up me or my Perfect Purse, which I'm wearing tonight with the crushed velvet cover.

"Everyone, over here," says Dad. We pile into a big booth in the back corner of the restaurant.

A waitress puts a basket of tortilla chips and some menus on the table. I take a chip with one hand and hold my purse with the other. I notice my purse is the exact same color as the tablecloth.

"Look Mom, it's a perfect match," I say waving my purse in front of her face.

But Mom doesn't look at my purse. She's

busy looking at the menu.

"Who wants tacos?" she asks.

All of Max's friends raise their hands.

"What about burritos?" says Mom.

All of Max's friends keep their hands up.
But I don't raise mine.

There's nothing wrong with tacos and
burritos, but there are so many things to
pick from on the menu at Casa Taco. I like
to try something new every time I come.

Mom orders a platter of tacos and a

platter of burritos for Max and his friends. "Mallory, what would you like?" Mom hands me a menu.

I try to open it, but it's hard. One hand is busy with chips. The other hand is holding a purse. What I need is an extra hand.

"You might want to put that purse down," says the waitress. "It will be easier to read the menu."

What I *don't* want to do is put my purse down. I don't want to get anything on it. Even though I love trying new things at Casa Taco, I don't even open the menu. I can't. "I'll just have tacos," I tell the waitress.

Mom finishes ordering while Dad stands up and tells us to move in closer for a picture. I hold my purse up in front of me while Dad snaps the picture.

When I sit back down, I keep holding my purse in front of me. I also go back to eating chips. I try dipping them in salsa, but it's not so easy to dip chips while you're holding a purse in the air.

Mom looks at me kind of funny. "Mallory, why don't you put your purse down on the bench?"

Maybe Mom doesn't want to look at my purse, but someone else might want to.

I think about Mary Ann. I know she wouldn't put her purse down on the bench, and I'm not going to either. "I'm OK," I tell Mom.

Mom shrugs. "Max, why don't you open your presents while we're waiting for the food," she says.

Max nods like he loves that idea.

"Open mine first," says Dylan. He shoves a red box in Max's direction.

Max takes it and rips the paper off. "A baseball glove! Cool!" he says to Dylan.

I know Max loves it. He's been wanting a new baseball glove.

Max puts his glove on his hand. "Think I can open presents with this on?" He scoops up a small box wrapped in blue paper with his gloved hand.

"That one's from Jared and Ben and Myles and me," says Brett.

"It must be good if it's from all four of

you," says Max. He tears the wrapping off of the box.

"Wow!" says Max, staring at what he's holding in his baseball glove. "A collector's edition of baseball cards! Thanks!"

I know Max would never hug his friends, but he looks like he's thinking about it.

"Open mine," says Adam. He gives Max a red envelope.

Max takes it from him and opens it up. When he sees what's inside, he high-fives Adam with his baseball glove. "Super cool! A gift certificate to Sports World."

"You can pick out anything you want," says Adam.

Max waves the envelope in the air. "Thanks," says Max.

"Maybe you'll like what's in this envelope too," says Dad. He hands Max a yellow envelope.

Max takes it from Dad and opens it. He smiles when he sees what's inside. "Twenty-five passes to go to the batting cages!" He takes them out so his friends can see.

I know Max is happy about that present. Going to the batting cages is his favorite thing to do.

"Thanks, everybody," Max says as he looks

around the table. "My presents are totally awesome!" Then he looks at me. "Mal, don't you have something too?" he asks.

I have something. I start to give the envelope I brought to Max, but then I stop.

"C'mon!" Max sticks his hand out. "I'm sure I'll like whatever you got me."

Maybe Max is sure he'll like what I got him, but I'm not. I hand Max the card I made and watch while Max opens it. There's something inside it, but I don't know if he will like it as much as he liked his other presents.

Max takes out the card I made and reads what I wrote. But he doesn't say a word.

"What is it?" asks Ben.

"A card," says Max.

"Is there anything else?" asks Jared.

"Yeah," says Max. He turns the envelope upside down and shakes it.

When he does, something else falls out, and that something else is glitter.

Max still doesn't say a word, so I say something. "It's not just a card! It's a present card."

"A present card?" says Brett, like he has

no clue what I'm talking about.

I take the card out of Max's hand. "This is not just a regular card."

I try to explain it the way Mary Ann and I talked about it, so everyone will understand. "This card is much, much, much more. It has glitter in it, and I cut it out in the shape of a baseball, which is Max's favorite sport."

I finish explaining and wait for everyone to nod their heads like they understand the difference between a present card and a regular card, but no one looks like they do.

"Is that all you got your brother for his birthday?" asks Dylan.

"I know what you should have given him," says Adam. "You should have given him a T-shirt that says '*All I got my brother for his birthday was this stinkin' card.*'" Adam points to the card I made.

All of Max's friends laugh, like they think what Adam suggested is hilarious. But Max isn't laughing. He's just sitting there quietly.

Max almost never just sits quietly, and I don't like when he does. Especially now.

Dad looks at Max's friends, who are still laughing. "Knock it off guys," he says.

They stop laughing, but it doesn't make me feel much better.

I look at my Perfect Purse sitting on the table next to the chip basket. I think back to the wish I made at the fountain in the mall. I wished somehow, some way, I would get the Perfect Purse.

Right now, I'd like to make a different wish. I'd wish that I could magically change my purse into a birthday present for my brother.

I put my purse down beside me on the

bench. I don't feel like looking at it right now, and I don't want anyone else to see it either.

When the waitress comes to the table with the food, she asks if we're ready for the fiesta. Everyone digs into the plates of food she put on the table . . . everyone but me.

I don't touch my tacos. Mom tries to pass me the platter of burritos, but I pass on those too. At cake time, all I do is pick at my piece.

When it's time to go, Dad takes all the boys in the van. "Mallory, do you want to ride with us?" he asks.

I shake my head *no*. The last thing I ever want to do is ride in a van filled with all of Max's friends. I get in the car with Mom.

She starts driving and then looks in the

rearview mirror. "You're awfully quiet."

I shrug my shoulders and look at my purse in my lap. I don't know what to say. I know Max liked his birthday, but I feel like I didn't do anything to make it special.

"Feel like talking?" asks Mom.

I shake my head again. I feel like Mom's eyes are staring inside me. I know what she wants to talk about, but it's not a conversation I want to have. Right now, I think riding in the van with the boys would be better than sitting in the same car with Mom.

When we get home, I start to go to my room. Mom stops me and hands me an envelope. "This came for you this afternoon," she says.

"Thanks," I mumble. I take the envelope and go to my room. It's a letter from Mary Ann.

Dear Mallory,

Hi! Hi! Hi!

This is just a quickie. But I have a V.I.Q.
VERY IMPORTANT QUESTION:

How do you like your purse? Have you
had so much fun carrying it? Which covers
have you used? Have you gotten tons of
compliments? Have you used the sparkly
pin yet? Isn't it cute?

I just love, love, love my Perfect Purse
and I hope you do too.

If you ask me, the Perfect Purse really is
perfect!

Big, happy hugs!
Mary Ann

P.S. How was Max's birthday party? Did
he love his card? Did you take your purse?
I bet you were the hit of the party!

I crumple up Mary Ann's letter and toss it into my trash. I pull Cheeseburger into my lap and stroke the fur on her back. "I know Mary Ann thinks the Perfect Purse is perfect," I say to my cat. "And maybe it is . . . for her."

But I'd like to give it a new name . . . the Not-So-Perfect Purse.

COUNTING
SHEEP

I turn onto my right side. I roll over onto my left. I lie on my back, close my eyes, and breathe deeply. I even try counting sheep. But no matter what I do, I can't fall asleep.

I pick up Cheeseburger and go upstairs to Mom and Dad's room. "I don't feel so good," I say when I walk into their room.

Mom sits up in bed and feels my head.

"You don't have a fever," she says.

"Does your throat hurt?" asks Dad.

I touch my throat. "No," I tell Dad. "My throat doesn't hurt."

"Is your nose stuffy?" asks Mom.

I sniffle and shake my head. "My nose isn't stuffy either."

Mom and Dad look at each other. "What do you think it is?" asks Dad.

I push my stomach in a few places. "It must be my stomach," I tell my parents. "Maybe I ate too much Mexican food."

Dad shakes his head. "I doubt that's it. You barely touched your dinner. Is anything bothering you?"

I shrug my shoulders. "Nothing is bothering me."

"Usually when I can't sleep it's because I've got something on my mind," says Mom. "Maybe you've got something on your mind."

I sit down on the bed. "The only thing on my mind is going to sleep."

Dad pats me on the head. "If that's the case, you need to get back into bed." He kisses me on the forehead. "You'll be fine."

I stand up and start walking back down the stairs to my room. But I don't feel like I'll be fine, and I don't think getting back into bed will help.

I turn around and go back to my parents' room. "I guess I do have something on my mind."

Dad pats the bed. "Why don't you sit down and tell us about it."

I sit down between Mom and Dad. I look down at the bed. "I feel bad about the card I gave Max. I feel like it wasn't a very good birthday present." I wait for Mom and Dad to say something, but they don't, so I keep talking.

"I should have used some of the money I made from the salon to get him a real present."

Mom looks at me like she thinks I should have too. "Mallory, how would you have felt if Max didn't give you a present on your birthday?"

I love getting presents, especially on my birthday. "Not so good," I mumble. But there's more to it than that. I try to explain so my parents will understand.

"I wanted to get Max a present. But then Mary Ann and I had the salon and we only made enough money to buy the purse. I felt like she would be really upset if I didn't get the purse. I didn't know what to do."

"Do you think you made the right decision?" asks Mom.

I think Mom already knows my answer, but I shake my head no anyway. Even though Mom thinks I made the wrong decision, I don't want her to think it was an easy one to make.

"It was hard to make the right decision, because when I was making it, Mary Ann reminded me that Max can be really mean to me sometimes."

"I agree with Mary Ann," says Mom.

I look up at Mom. "You do?" I can't believe Mom agrees with Mary Ann. She almost never agrees with her.

"Yes," says Mom. "Max should be nicer. But two wrongs don't make a right."

"Huh?" I say. Mom's math makes no sense to me.

"What I mean is that if Max does something wrong, it's not OK for you to do something wrong too." Mom has on her teacher face. "If someone does something to you that you don't like, it doesn't make it right for you to do something they might not like back. Do you understand?"

I nod my head. "I get what you're saying." Then I stop nodding. "It's not just that I feel bad about not getting Max a present, something else is bothering me too."

Dad looks surprised. "Mallory, what is it?" he asks.

I take a deep breath. It's a lot of things, and I tell them all to Mom and Dad.

"I was really excited to get the purse, and now that I have it, it's not as great as I thought it would be. I couldn't take it to school. It wasn't fun to take it to a restaurant. I didn't get a present for Max because I got the purse instead. And Joey's upset because I haven't played with him for a long time because I've been busy trying to buy the purse.

"I was really excited to have the same purse as Mary Ann. We always like having the same things, and she loves having it, but I don't think it's been much fun."

When I finish talking, Dad starts.

"Maybe you and Mary Ann don't *always* like having the same things," says Dad.

"Maybe you just like having the same things *some* of the time. You're two different people, and you have to do what works for you."

I don't say a word, but I know what Dad says is true. He keeps talking. "As for Joey, he's a good friend. I bet if you explain things to him, he'll understand."

I nod my head. "I'm sure Joey will understand." Lately, I think he's been a better friend to me than I've been to him. I look down at my hands. "What about Max? I let Mary Ann talk me into not getting him a present, and now I feel awful about that."

Dad tilts my chin up so I'm looking him in the eyes. "Mallory, you have a brother and Mary Ann doesn't. It's probably hard for her to understand how you feel about having a brother because she's never had one."

"I never thought of that," I say to Dad.

I hang my head.

"Mallory," says Dad, "life is full of decisions. Sometimes making them is complicated. No one can make your decisions for  you. As you get older, it is up to you to make good decisions."

Even though I love getting older, there are parts of it that aren't so much fun. "I feel like I made some bad decisions and there's nothing I can do about it."

"Mallory," says Mom, "you can't take the purse back, but there are lots of nice things you can do for Max. And I'm sure you can find a way to patch things up with Joey.

Why don't you give it some thought, and I'm sure you'll come up with something."

"I'll try," I tell Mom. I scoop up Cheeseburger, kiss my parents good night, and go back downstairs to my room.

When I get into bed, I make a wish.

I wish my brain will think of something nice to do for Max and Joey.

THE PERFECT PRESENT

Some people do their best thinking in the middle of the night, and I must be one of those people. I thought of something great at exactly 3:22 a.m.

I look at my clock. Now it's 7:30 a.m. Time to put Operation *Do-Something-Nice-for-Max's-Birthday* into place.

I knock on his door and then open it

before he has a chance to tell me I can't come in. "I have something for you," I tell my brother.

"Whatever," grumbles Max.

He's been grumbling at me ever since we left Casa Taco last night.

I ignore the grumbling. "I think you're going to like it," I say as I walk into his room. I hand him an envelope with his name on it. "It's a belated birthday present."

Max rolls his eyes. "It's a card," he says like he's already gotten one card from me that wasn't so great, and he doesn't think getting a second one will be much better.

"Open it!" I tell him.

Max opens the envelope, pulls out the card, and starts reading. "This card entitles the birthday boy, Max McDonald, to one day of labor from his loving sister, Mallory McDonald."

"Not this again," groans Max. "I thought you were getting out of the girl for hire business."

I grin. "The only business I'm in is the birthday business," I tell Max. "My belated birthday present to you is that I'm going to work for you for a day, and you don't even have to hire me."

Now it's Max's turn to grin. "Great! When do we start?"

I bow to my brother, like I'm his servant. "There's no time like the present for a present!"

Max plops down in his desk chair and props his feet up on the desk. "Why don't you start with the bed."

I look at Max, then at the pile of messed up blankets. I take a deep breath. Working for him won't be easy. I pull up covers while Max sits in his chair and watches.

Then he gets up and leaves. When he comes back, he has Mom's camera in his hand. "I've got to get pictures of this." He snaps a photo of me fluffing his pillows.

When Max's bed is made, he points to the closet. "My shoes are a mess."

I look in Max's closet. His shoes are everywhere! I start picking up sneakers and looking for mates. Max takes more pictures.

When I have all his shoes lined up in pairs, Max looks at his watch. "I'm supposed to take out the trash now."

I think about all the times I've seen Max lugging those heavy bags outside. I don't really want to do this job, but I did tell Max I would work for him for a day.

I follow Max down the hall and into the kitchen. Mom and Dad are sitting at the table reading the newspaper. "Good morning, you two," says Mom.

"Good morning," I say. I reach under the sink to get a twisty tie for the garbage bag. I close up the garbage bag and start pulling the bag out of the trash can.

Dad clears his throat. "Max, isn't it your job to take out the trash?"

Max takes a bowl of grapes out of the refrigerator and sits down. He pops a grape into his mouth. "It is my job," he

says, "but today, Mallory is doing my jobs."
He takes a picture of me picking up the
garbage bag.

Mom looks at Max like he should be doing
his own jobs. "Max, what's going on? Why is
Mallory doing your jobs? And why are you
taking pictures of her doing them?"

"I can explain," I say. "I want to do
Max's jobs."

Mom and Dad look at each other, but
they look confused.

"It's a belated birthday gift," I say in my
remember-what-we-talked-about-last-night voice.

Mom and Dad nod, like they get it.
"How nice," Mom says to Max.

Max nods like he agrees and pops
another grape into his mouth.

When I come back into the kitchen
from taking the trash out, I pour a glass
of orange juice. I drink it in one gulp.

Working for Max is a lot of . . . *work!*

"What do I do now?" I ask my brother.

"Follow me," says Max.

I walk behind him into the bathroom we share. "It's my day to clean the bathroom." Max hands me the toilet scrubber.

I guess that means it's *my* day to clean the bathroom. I look under the sink for the toilet bowl cleaner. I pour some in. While I swish it around with the scrubber, Max takes pictures.

I flush, then Max and I watch the little scrubby bubbles go down the toilet together. When the noise stops, Max looks in the bowl. "Are you ready to sweep the garage?" he asks.

"Ready as I'll ever be. But no more pictures, OK?"

Max agrees, and I head outside. When I come back inside, he gives me a handwritten list of chores.

When I'm done with everything on the list, I go into Max's room to see what else he wants me to do. But his answer surprises me. "You've done enough," he says.

I rub my ears, like maybe I didn't hear Max right. "You don't want me to do anything else?"

"Nope." Max shakes his head.

Oh no! I hope Max liked his present. "Was everything OK?" I ask.

"Everything was great," he says. Then he stretches, like he's tired. "I'm going to go lie down on my freshly made bed."

I start to go into my room, but Max stops me.

"Hey Mal," he says. "Thanks for my birthday present. I really liked it."

"You're welcome," I tell my brother. I'm glad he liked his present. Even though it was hard work, I liked giving it to him.

I go into my room and shut the door.
I take a sheet of paper out of my desk.

Dear Mary Ann,
Sit down when you read this! If you
read it standing, you might faint!

Today, I went to work for Max!
I know, you're probably wondering
how Max got me to work for him. You're
probably thinking I didn't even get paid.
But here's the part that might make
you faint . . . it was my idea to work for
Max, and I didn't even make him pay me.
Don't worry! I didn't eat any poisonous
berries that made me go crazy. I worked
for Max as a present.
I decided he needed something to go

with the card. You know how much we
like it when we get something to go with
the cards! Well, I decided, he would too.

And he did.

The thing is, I felt awful not getting
him a birthday gift. (I know . . . how could
I feel awful about anything that has to
do with Max, but I did.)

Even though he can be mean to me,
he's still my brother. He always gives me
something on my birthday and I wanted
to give him something on his.

And I'm glad I did. I could tell he liked
getting a present from me.

One other thing: I know you love,
love, love having the Perfect Purse, but I
haven't loved having it all that much.

The Perfect Purse is really cute. But it
took a lot to get it, and then once I got it, I
didn't think it was that much fun to have it.

I know we always love the same things, but this time I think I loved it less than you did. I guess best friends, even lifelong ones, don't always like the same things.

Except for *Fashion Fran*. Our favorite show starts at five o'clock. Talk to you then!

Big Huge Hugs and Kisses,
Mallory

When I finish the letter, I put it in an envelope to Mary Ann and go outside to put it in the mailbox. Even though I've done a lot today, there's one more thing I need to do.

I grab something off my desk, then I walk next door to Joey's.

KNOCK, KNOCK

Knock. Knock. I knock on the Winstons' front door with one hand and keep my other hand behind my back.

"Who's there?" asks a familiar voice.

"Mallory."

Joey opens his front door and looks at me like I'm someone he hasn't seen for a long time. "Mallory who?" he asks.

"Ha, ha!" I say smiling. "Very funny."

But Joey doesn't look like he thinks it's

funny at all.

"I know I haven't been a very good friend lately," I say to him before he has a chance to say anything to me. "And I'm really sorry."

Joey is quiet, so I keep talking.

"Having the Perfect Purse isn't nearly as much fun as spending time with my friend," I say to Joey.

I look at him when I say it. Joey says OK, like everything is OK now that I've explained things. But I know Joey, and I know everything is not OK.

"I brought you something," I say to him. I give Joey what I've been holding behind my back.

He looks down at what I'm holding in front of him. "Wow!" A big smile spreads across his face. "You don't have to give me that."

"I want to,"
I tell him.

"But it's your
favorite joke
book," he says.

I look down
at the book
in my hand.
"Maybe you're
right," I say to Joey like the idea of giving
away my favorite book is really crazy.
"Maybe I should keep it."

The smile on Joey's face disappears.

Then I start laughing. "Just joking!" I say.
I stick the book in his hands. "Why don't
you go put that in your room and get your
skateboard."

The smile on Joey's face reappears. "I'll
be right back," he says.

TOP SECRET PHOTOS

The only thing worse than working for Max for a day are these pictures that he took of me working for him for a day.

I am showing them to you for one reason: If you don't see these pictures of me working for Max, you will never see any other pictures of me working for Max because I am never working for him again!

You have to promise, promise, promise not to show these to anyone else!

Max's shoes smell worse than Cheeseburger's litter box!

Even the garbage smells better!

And so does the toilet!

REMEMBER: THESE ARE FOR YOUR EYES ONLY . . . YOU PROMISED!

Some Beautiful News

By Jackson Cole

If you look around the halls of Fern Falls Elementary, you will notice that girls in Mrs. Daily's third-grade class are looking more beautiful than ever. They are wearing the latest hairstyles and the newest nail and makeup colors.

Where did they all get so fashionable, you might ask?

The answer is easy. They went to *Salon Mallory*, the newest hair salon for girls to open in Fern Falls. *Salon Mallory* is located at 17 Wish Pond Road in the room of Fern Falls Elementary third-grader, Mallory McDonald.

We had a chance to catch up with Miss McDonald, following the grand opening of her salon, and here's what she had to say:

"Making money is hard work, but deciding what to do with it is even harder."

Miss McDonald wishes to thank her business partner (and lifelong best friend) Mary Ann for helping to make the salon a reality.

She also wishes to inform the
public that *Salon Mallory* is
temporarily closed for business.
But she says if you need help with
your hair, just stop by her desk
at school. She's happy to give out
free pointers.

We asked Miss McDonald if she
has any advice for other kids
starting a business. She says the

key is to find something you like
doing, and then have fun doing it.

   Miss McDonald wants to wish
anyone who is thinking about
starting their own business the
best, best, best of luck!

Darby Creek
A division of Lerner Publishing Group, Inc.
241 First Avenue North
Minneapolis, MN 55401 U.S.A.

Website address: www.lernerbooks.com

Library of Congress Cataloging-in-Publication Data

Friedman, Laurie B.
    In business with mallory / by Laurie Friedman ; illustrations by Barbara Pollak.
        p.   cm.
    Summary: When mallory's mother refuses to buy her a purse, mallory tries a series of businesses in order to make money and buy it herself.
    ISBN 978-1-57505-925-9 (lib. bdg. : alk. paper)
    ISBN 978-0-8225-6536-9 (eBook)
    [1. Handbags—Fiction. 2. moneymaking projects—Fiction.] I. Pollak, Barbara, ill.
II. Title.
PZ7.F89773Inab 2006
[Fic]—dc22   2005020620

Heart to Heart with mallory

For Beth Ertel—Happy Birthday!
Big huge hugs and Kisses!
—L. F.

For Cole and miranda
—B. P.

Heart to Heart with Mallory

by Laurie Friedman

illustrations by Barbara Pollak

darbycreek

MINNEAPOLIS

CONTENTS

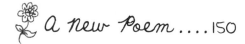

A WORD FROM MALLORY

This morning, I found two strange things in the mailbox. One was an invitation. The other was a package.

First, let me tell you about the invitation. It was addressed to my whole family, and it was from my next door neighbor, Mr. Winston. He invited Mom and Dad and Max and me to a Valentine's party. And the invitation said: Dress Fancy.

Now, you're probably thinking that's nice because parties are lots of fun. But trust me when I tell you it's strange too, because ever since I moved to Wish Pond Road, I've never known Mr. Winston to throw a party. Even Joey, my on-the-street best friend,

6

would tell you that his dad isn't exactly the party-throwing type.

Strange, huh? But wait till you hear about the package. It's even stranger.

My grandma sent me a diary, and she sent it with a note that said: Dear Honey Bee, You can tell your deepest thoughts and feelings to your diary. Love, Grandma.

When I read the note, I called Grandma and reminded her that I didn't need to tell my deepest thoughts and feelings to a diary because I have a best friend for that.

But Grandma said there might be some things I can't tell Mary Ann. And she said it in an I-know-things-that-you-don't sort of way.

All of a sudden, Mr. Winston is throwing a fancy party, and Grandma thinks there are things I can't tell my best friend. Think what you want, but I think things are getting a little strange around here.

And I'm not sure I like it.

This is the

Top-Secret

Diary

of Mallory

McDonald

TOP SECRET

Winston
Wish Pond Rd

The McDonalds
17 Wish Pond Road

AN iNViTaTion

✿ The favour of a reply is requested by February 10

_____

_____   ○ will attend
                             ○ cannot attend

total number of people _____

MY LOVE   MARRY ME

An Invitation

Dear Diary,

I haven't even started writing in you and it already feels weird.

Whenever I write "Dear" anything, it's always Dear Mary Ann. But since Grandma gave you to me as a gift, I feel like I have to fill up these pages. I hope I don't hurt your feelings if I tell you that's not something I really want to do.

But the thing is, I have something to tell you. Actually, I have something to show you, and that something is an invitation. It's from Mr. Winston. He's having a Valentine's Party. Wait till you see the invitation! Mr. Winston wrote a mushy poem about LOVE!

If you ask me, it's very "un" Mr. Winston, but I don't care. I love parties (especially the kind where you get to dress up) and I can't wait to go to this one.

♥ *Mallory*

P.S. I can't decide if I should wear my pink skirt with the ruffly top or my red dress with hearts on it.

Ruffles? <u>OR</u> Hearts?

P.P.S. The good news: I have three weeks to decide because that's when the party is. The bad news: I have to wait three weeks for the party to get here. (Boo Hoo! I hate to wait!)

Love is...

Love is like a flower, beautiful and rare.

Love is a special feeling, none other can compare.

Love is a magician, cloaked in mystery.

Love can help illuminate things we can not see.

Love is a fuzzy sweater; it warms us deep inside.

Love is all around us; it leaves no place to hide.

Love is a precious gift; simple, clear and true.

Love is at its best when it reaches out for you.

By Frank Winston

Please join me for a celebration of love.

Date: Valentine's Day

Place: The Winston House,
15 Wish Pond Road

Time: 7 p.m.

R.S.V.P. Frank, Winnie, Joey,
or Grandpa Winston

Dress: Fancy!

SATURDAY AFTERNOON, AT MY DESK

Dear Diary,

Don't you just love, love, LOVE that invitation? I can't wait to tell Mary Ann about the party!

♡ *Mallory*

SATURDAY AFTERNOON, BACK AT MY DESK

Dear Diary,

Guess what? I don't have to tell Mary Ann about the party. She already knows about it because she's invited too!

Listen to this. After lunch, I was skateboarding with Joey when he said to me, "Hey, did you know Mary Ann is coming to visit in three weeks?"

So I said, "Mary Ann's not coming to

visit in three weeks. I'm her best friend. Don't you think I would know if she was?"

But Joey kept on skateboarding and when he was about to jump a rock, he said, "She is coming. And so is her mom. They're coming for the Valentine's party that my dad is throwing."

When Joey said that, I stopped skateboarding. I put my foot on the rock that Joey was about to jump so he had to stop too. "Really?" I said to him like "Is

TELL ME WHAT YOU KNOW!

I didn't do...

that really true and can you tell me more?"

And Joey did.

"I heard my dad on the phone with Mary Ann's mom this morning," he said. "He asked her if she'd found a dress for the party yet. Then he said he can't wait to see what she's going to wear."

That's when Joey went back to skateboarding. But not me. How could I keep skateboarding when my mind was busy filling up with questions like:

Why would Mr. Winston be talking on the phone to Mary Ann's mom?

Why would he invite Mary Ann and her mom to his party?

And why would he care what Mary Ann's mom is wearing to the party?

So I asked Joey another question that was on my mind. "Hey Joey, I know your dad and Mary Ann's mom have been out on a few dates, but do they talk on the phone a lot?"

Joey stopped skateboarding and looked at me. "Define a lot," he said.

"Talking on the phone to someone every day is a lot," I said to Joey.

And when I said that, Joey laughed. He said he thinks his dad talks to Mary Ann's mom at least ten times a day. He said that every time he walks into his house, that's what his dad is doing.

Now I know what I need to be doing, and that is getting some answers. I want to know why Mr. Winston is spending all his time on the phone with Mary Ann's mom.

♡ *Mallory*

SATURDAY NIGHT, ON THE COUCH WITH MY FAVORITE BABYSITTER

Dear Diary,

I began my search for answers tonight. I started with my babysitter, Crystal.

She says she's good at knowing things about people. Sometimes when she babysits, she brings a little crystal ball with her. She says when she looks into it, she gets the answers she's looking for.

So tonight, I asked her if she would please look into her crystal ball and get an answer for me. I asked her if she could tell me what's going on between Joey's dad and Mary Ann's mom.

Crystal looked into her crystal ball. Then she said she needed more information.

So I gave her some.

"It's like this," I explained to her. "First, Mary Ann's mom came here to visit, and she went out on a date with Joey's dad. They had a good time, so they went out on more dates. Now, Joey's father, who never throws parties, is throwing a fancy Valentine's party, and he invited Mary Ann and her mom. And he's spending all of his time talking on the phone to her."

When I finished giving Crystal this information, I told her to look into her crystal ball and give me my answer.

But she said she didn't need a crystal ball to answer this question. "It sounds to me like they're in love," she said.

"Please look into your ball and make sure you're right," I said to Crystal.

So she looked, then she nodded her head like she was sure she knew what she was talking about.

But there's only one thing I'm sure about ... and that's that Crystal needs a new crystal ball.

♡ *Mallory*

BAD BALL

<u>SUNDAY MORNING, AT THE BREAKFAST TABLE WITH MOM AND DAD AND MAX AND A BOX OF CHOCOLATE DOUGHNUT HOLES</u>

Dear Diary,

This morning, while Max was eating chocolate doughnut holes and Mom and Dad were reading the newspaper, I walked into the kitchen.

"Mallory, would you like a doughnut

hole?" Dad asked me.

But I told him I didn't want a doughnut hole. What I wanted was an answer. "Mom, Dad," I asked. "Are Mary Ann's mom and Joey's dad in love?"

When I asked that, Mom put down her coffee cup and gave Dad a look. Dad gave her a look back. "They enjoy each other's company," Mom said.

That didn't sound like much of an answer to me. "Does that mean they're in love?" I asked.

"It means they'd like to spend more time together," said Dad.

That didn't sound like an answer either.

So I asked my question again. A little louder. "CAN SOMEBODY PLEASE TELL ME, AND TELL ME NOW, IF MARY ANN'S MOM AND JOEY'S DAD ARE IN LOVE?"

And when I asked it like that, I got an answer. "Yes, Mallory," said Mom. "Mary Ann's mom and Joey's dad are in love."

And even though Mom answered my question, it made me have a whole lot more.

Like how can they be in love if they live in different cities? And why would they be in love anyway? And are they planning to go off and get married and live happily ever after just like people do on TV?

When I asked those questions, Mom and Dad smiled at each other. But I guess I didn't look like I was in the mood for them to smile, because Dad stopped smiling and started explaining.

He told me that it would be more convenient if they lived in the same place, but that all it means is that they will have to work a little harder at planning to see each other.

Then he said it's always difficult to explain why two people love each other, but that Joey's dad and Mary Ann's mom have a lot in common and enjoy being together.

Then Dad told me that he didn't know if they would get married, that we'd all have to just wait and see.

There's just one problem: I'm scared if I wait I won't like what I'm going to see.

♡ *Mallory*

SUNDAY NIGHT, SITTING AT MY DESK WITH CHEESEBURGER

Dear Diary,

I keep thinking about my conversation this morning with Mom and Dad. I know I'm not the wait-and-see type.

I know something else too.

I know what Grandma meant when she said there might be some things I can't tell Mary Ann. She thinks I can't tell Mary Ann that it's NOT a good idea for her mom and Joey's dad to be in love.

But Grandma is wrong about that. I CAN tell Mary Ann and I KNOW she will agree. Mary Ann and I agree on just about everything.

I'm going to call Mary Ann right now and get this whole thing straightened out.

 Mallory

See! We agree on <u>everything</u>!

<u>SUNDAY NIGHT, 6:36,</u>
<u>AT THE PHONE IN THE KITCHEN</u>

Dear Diary,

I just tried to call Mary Ann. Her line
is busy.

♡ *Mallory*

SUNDAY NIGHT, 6:52, STILL AT THE PHONE IN THE KITCHEN

Dear Diary,

I just tried again.

Her line is still busy.

♡ *Mallory*

beep! beep! beep!

7:11

STILL BUSY! I wonder who is on the phone at Mary Ann's house.

♡ *Mallory*

7:48

Dear Diary,

I just got back from Joey's house.

I went over there to return a comic book I borrowed from Joey.

But that's not why I really went.

I wanted to see what the Winstons were doing. Here's what I found out: Joey and Winnie were doing their homework, Grandpa Winston was reading a book, and guess what Mr. Winston was doing? HE WAS ON THE PHONE!

♡ *Mallory*

7:53
Dear Diary,
I just called Mary Ann again. Her line is still busy. I think I know who is on the phone.

♡ *Mallory*

8:11
Still busy.

<u>8:22</u>
Still busy.

<u>8:29</u>
Dear Diary,
I bet you think I'm going to write "Still busy." But you're wrong. I don't Know if Mary Ann's phone is still busy because Mom won't let me call again to find out. She says I have to go to bed.
♡ *Mallory*

<u>SUNDAY NIGHT, IN MY BED</u>
<u>WITH CHEESEBURGER</u>
Dear Diary,
With all due respect (I have always wanted to use these words even though they don't make much sense), I can't

fall asleep.

I wish I could have talked to Mary Ann tonight. But the first thing I'm going to do when I get home from school tomorrow is call her.

I don't like this whole Mary Ann's-mom-talking-all-night-on-the-phone-with-Joey's-dad thing. It's keeping me from sleeping.

♡ *Mallory*

P.S. Writing in a journal in the dark while you're holding a flashlight is not easy to do, but this is the last time I will have to do it because after I call Mary Ann tomorrow and straighten this whole thing out, I won't have anymore sleepless nights.

A Trip

Dear Diary,

We hardly know each other, but I'm going to tell you something private.

I have an EMERGENCY! (Not a medical emergency, a Mallory Emergency!)

Someone is going on a trip and that someone is not me.

Here's how I found out:

Right when I got home from school, I called Mary Ann. I told her I had something BIG to tell her. I was going to tell her how I thought it was a bad idea about her mom and Joey's dad being in love, and how I knew she would think so too.

But before we even started talking

31

about that, Mary Ann said she had something HUGE to tell me. She told me that Joey is going on a trip to visit her!

You probably think you're hearing things, because that's what I thought when I heard her say it. So I'll say it again.

JOEY IS GOING TO VISIT MARY ANN!!!!!!!!!!!

Can you believe it? I can't!

Four days from now, Joey and his dad, and his sister, Winnie, are going to see Mary Ann and her mom for the weekend. Four days from now, they will be going to my old neighborhood to see my best friend.

When Mary Ann finished telling me her huge news, she asked me what my big news was. But hearing her huge news made me not want to tell her my big news. So I told her I forgot what I was going to say. Then I hung up the phone.

♡ *Mallory*

P.S. I was so surprised when Mary Ann told me Joey and Winnie are going to visit her that I didn't even ask why they're going to visit. I'm going to go call Mary Ann back right now. I'm sure there is a very good explanation for all of this.

STILL AT THE KITCHEN DESK, 10 MINUTES LATER

Dear Diary,

The good news: there is an explanation for why the Winstons are going to visit Mary Ann.

The bad news: the explanation stinks.

Here it is: When I asked Mary Ann why Joey and Winnie and Mr. Winston would be going to visit her, she told me that they're going to visit her and her mom because her mom and Joey's dad are IN LOVE!

She said her mom said they want to spend lots more time getting to know each other and each other's families.

And that's not all she said.

She said that now that her mom is in love, she gets to have toaster waffles and chocolate milk for dinner and stay up past her bedtime.

She said the reason for that is because her mom is so busy talking on the phone to Joey's dad that she doesn't spend a lot of time cooking for her or remembering her bedtime.

But Mary Ann said she's glad because

she loves toaster waffles and hates going to bed. Then, Mary Ann said one more thing. She said now that her mom and Joey's dad are in love, she gets to call Mr. Winston by his first name, Frank.

I can just hear her:

Frank, isn't it a beautiful day?

Frank, would you like to see me ride my bike?

Frank, can you please pass the meatballs?

I can't believe she gets to do this! I have known "Frank" much longer than she has, and I still have to call him Mr. Winston.

♡ *Mallory*

P.S. In case you're wondering how my I-don't-think-it's-a-great-idea-for-your-mom-and-Joey's-dad-to-be-in-

love-and-I-know-you'll-agree-because-
we-agree-on-everything talk went with
Mary Ann... DON'T!

Grandma was right. There are some
things I can't tell Mary Ann.

MONDAY NIGHT, IN MY BED (JUST BACK FROM MOM AND DAD'S BED)

Dear Diary,

I couldn't sleep. I tried counting sheep
and cats and dogs and pigs. I even tried

singing myself to sleep, but Max came
into my room and told me that if I
said one more word I'd be
sleeping outside
(and he didn't say
it very nicely).

When he said
that, I scooped up
Cheeseburger and
went upstairs to Mom
and Dad's room and told
them I would have to sleep
with them tonight.

But they said I had to
sleep in my own room. So
I told them what I've been thinking
ever since this afternoon.

I told them they haven't been very
good parents lately.

When I said that, they acted shocked

and surprised. They said, "Mallory, can you please tell us what in the world you're talking about?"

So I did. "Mom, Dad, why didn't you tell me about the Winstons' trip to see Mary Ann and her mom?"

"Mallory," said Mom, "I just found out about the trip today."

"So why didn't you tell me when you found out?" I asked.

Then Mom and Dad started talking at the same time:

I WAS GOING TO TELL YOU, BUT MARY ANN TOLD YOU FIRST.

MALLORY, YOU ARE OVERREACTING!

So I told Mom and Dad that I wasn't overreacting. Then I told them about an expression that Mrs. Daily taught us at school. It's called "keeping people in the loop" and it means telling them what's going on.

I told them I wanted them to keep me in the loop, especially when it comes to Frank and Colleen.

Mom and Dad said they would be happy to keep me in the loop and that anytime I have a question I should feel free to ask them.

So I said I had another one.

"How come Mary Ann gets to call Mr. Winston Frank, and I have to call him Mr. Winston?" I asked Mom and Dad.

They said this was a very good question and that they didn't have an answer for it.

I asked if they could please get me
one soon.
♡ *Mallory*

TUESDAY, AFTER SCHOOL
Dear Diary,
It's official. I now call Mr. Winston
Frank. Just like Mary Ann.
I'm going next door. To say "hi" to Frank.
♡ *Mallory*

TUESDAY AFTERNOON, BACK FROM FRANK'S HOUSE
Dear Diary,
I didn't get to say
"hi" to Frank. He was
on the phone.

WHO IS FRANK
TALKING TO?

But I did talk to Joey and Winnie, and I learned three new things.

New thing #1: Joey and Winnie don't have to go to school on Friday, because they're leaving early that morning to go see Mary Ann and her mom.

New thing #2: They are doing a lot of fun things this weekend. Friday night, they're going out for pizza and to see a movie. Saturday, they're going rollerblading. And Saturday night, they're going to an amusement park.

New thing #3: Joey and Winnie are going to call Mary Ann's mom Colleen.

In case you're wondering why they're going to call her Colleen, it's because Colleen is her first name.

♡ Mallory

P.S. Winnie told me she gets to buy a new sweater and jeans just for next weekend. She said her dad understood when she told him she wants to look extra special because it's going to be an extra-special weekend. If you ask me, she made up an "extra-special" excuse just to get new clothes.

TUESDAY NIGHT, IN MY BED

Dear Diary,

The only things I can think about are Joey and Winnie and Mary Ann at the amusement park. I think about them on the ferris wheel and the roller coaster. I think about them eating cotton candy and popcorn. I think about them laughing and talking and having a good time.

Diary, I do not like thinking about these things.

♡ *Mallory*

P.S. Do you think it's mean of me to think about Winnie getting cotton candy on her new sweater?

Oh no!
My new sweater!

WEDNESDAY AFTER SCHOOL, AT THE WISH POND

Dear Diary,

Today at school, all Joey talked about was his trip.

After school, all Max talked about was how lucky I am to be getting rid of Joey for a weekend. How come I don't feel lucky?

Mallory

"We're Having Fun!"

NOT ME!

WEDNESDAY NIGHT, IN MY BED

Dear Diary,

Tonight at dinner, while Mom and Dad and Max were eating Moo Shue Chicken, I made a decision. I'm going to ask Frank if I can go with them this weekend to visit Mary Ann and her mom.

There's another expression that Mrs. Daily taught us at school. It's called "the more the merrier" and it means the more people that you have to do something, the more fun things will be. I am going to tell Frank that the more people that go on this trip, the more fun it will be.

I think Mrs. Daily will be very proud of me when she sees how I am using what she has taught us.

♡ *Mallory*

P.S. I know Frank will say "yes." What else could he say?

THURSDAY MORNING
BEFORE SCHOOL

mom says I can't ask Frank if I can go on the trip.

THURSDAY AFTERNOON
AFTER SCHOOL

mom is mad at me.

I asked Frank if I can go on the trip.

mom says she told me not to ask, but I told her I forgot.

Then mom said she didn't believe I forgot and that starting Friday after school, I am going to be spending some

MAD MUM!

time in my room.

I guess I couldn't have gone on the trip anyway.

♡ *Mallory*

FRIDAY AFTER SCHOOL, IN MY ROOM

Dear Diary,

Joey was not in school today. The Winstons' car is not in their driveway.

Wish Pond Road is very, very, very quiet.

The only sound I hear is Cheeseburger snoring.

♡ *Mallory*

SATURDAY MORNING,
BACK FROM THE WINSTONS'

Dear Diary,

When I woke up, I do what I do every Saturday morning. I got dressed, ate breakfast, and went over to Joey's house.

You're probably wondering why I would do that since Joey's not even there. But the person I wanted to talk to this morning was not Joey. It was Grandpa Winston. I wanted to find out if Joey and Winnie are having a LOT of fun or just a little bit of fun with Mary Ann.

Here's what I found out: Grandpa Winston had no idea!

He said he had no idea because no one has called him to tell him how the trip is going. He said it's a good sign that everyone is having so much fun that they

haven't had time to call home. Personally,
I don't think it's a good sign at all.

♡ *Mallory*

SATURDAY AFTERNOON, ALONE

Dear Diary,

There is no one to play with. Max
said he doesn't want to skateboard with
me. Grandpa Winston said he doesn't
know how.

SUNDAY AFTERNOON, 2:19, LOOKING OUT MY WINDOW

Dear Diary,

I'm waiting for Joey and Winnie and Frank to get home.

Dad said they should be home sometime this afternoon.

I'm going to wait right here until I see their car in their driveway. When I do, I'm going to go next door and see if they had a good time with Mary Ann.

♡ *Mallory*

2:38

Still no car in the Winstons' driveway.

3:18

Still no car. I'm going to take a bathroom break.

B.R.B. (Be right back.)

4:48

Dear Diary,

I took a bathroom break. I took a washing-my-hands break. I took a feeding-Cheeseburger break. I took an eating-leftover-doughnut-holes break. I even took a watching-a-baseball-game-that-I-didn't-want-to-watch-with-Dad-and-Max break.

STILL NO CAR IN THE WINSTONS' DRIVEWAY!

♡ Mallory

<u>5:11</u>

Dear Diary,

Guess what? NO CAR! I'm sick of waiting. I have more important things to do. I'm going to go rearrange my hair thingies drawer.

♡ *Mallory*

<u>6:59</u>

Dear Diary,

Since I finished dinner, four things have happened:

1. I opened my curtains and looked out my window, and right when I did, I saw the Winstons' car pulling into their driveway.

2. I watched Winnie and Joey unloading their car and they each had something: A stuffed bear (like the kind

you win at an amusement park).

3. I closed my curtains so they couldn't see me looking at them.

4. I made a decision. I'm not going to ask Joey if he had a fun weekend. I mean, it really doesn't matter to me one way or the other if he had a fun weekend. I'm DEFINITELY not going to ask him. I don't even care if he did.

♡ *Mallory*

FOR A GREAT WEEKEND, GO TO AN AMUSEMENT PARK AND LEAVE YOUR BEST FRIEND AT HOME.

a Secret

MONDAY AFTER SCHOOL, AT MY DESK WITH CHEESEBURGER

Dear Diary,

I know a secret. I bet you want to know what it is. It's a long story, but I'll tell you.

It started this morning when I didn't walk to school with Joey like I always do. I didn't walk with him because I didn't want to hear about his weekend with Mary Ann.

But for some reason, right when I got to school, the first thing I asked Joey was if he had a fun weekend with Mary Ann.

Really, I didn't ask him. My mouth did. It just sort of started talking before I could stop it and here's what it said:

Mallory: So, how was your weekend with Mary Ann?

Joey: Fun.

Mallory: What did you do?

Joey: We went for pizza, rollerblading, and to an amusement park.

Mallory: Is that all?

Joey: Yep.

Mallory: You're not leaving anything out?

Joey: Nope.

And that made me wonder. I mean, how could Joey not be leaving something out? He was there for a whole weekend. So I asked what I really wanted to know. I asked him what it was like hanging out with Mary Ann and her mom.

And Joey said, "OK, I guess."

Then Joey said something that

surprised me. He said he wanted to do his math.

The weird thing about that is that Joey never wants to do his math. So I did some math of my own. "YEP" and "NOPE" and "OK, I guess" just didn't add up.

"YEP" + "NOPE" + "OK, I guess" = A phone call to Mary Ann

Something told me that there was something Joey did NOT want to tell me and I knew that if I wanted to find out, I was going to have to ask someone else.

♡ Mallory

P.S. If you're still wondering what the secret is, stay tuned. I'm about to tell you.

MONDAY NIGHT,
ON THE FLOOR OF THE BATHROOM
I SHARE WITH MAX

Dear Diary,

I had to lock myself in the bathroom so no one can see what I'm writing.

What I'm writing is V.I.S. That's short for Very Important Stuff, and Mary Ann told me lots of it.

When I called Mary Ann to see how the weekend was with the Winstons, she told me she had one great thing, one not-so-great thing, and one big secret to tell me.

Even though I couldn't wait to hear the big secret, I was kind of scared to. So I asked Mary Ann to start with the not-so-great thing. She told me that Joey and his dad were really nice, but that Winnie barely spoke to her all weekend.

I told Mary Ann that Winnie barely

speaks to anybody and when she does, whatever she says isn't nice at all.

Then, Mary Ann told me the great thing, and you won't believe what she told me.

She told me that her mom and Joey's dad aren't just in love, they are head-over-heels in love.

I knew what she meant when she said that because Mrs. Daily taught us the expression "head-over-heels." She said that it usually refers to love and it means when two people are crazy about each other.

So I asked Mary Ann how she knew that her mom and Joey's dad are head-over-heels for each other. Mary Ann said she knows because her mom calls Frank, "my Frank" and Frank calls her mom, "my Colleen."

When Mary Ann told me that, I told her that just because they say stuff like that doesn't mean they're head-over-heels.

Then, Mary Ann told me there's more. She said that when Frank left, she heard him tell her mom that when they're not together, he's "filled with despair," and her mom said she felt exactly the same way.

I didn't actually know what that meant, so I asked Mary Ann, who said she asked her mom the same question and her mom said that it's when you're completely sad about something.

Then Mary Ann told me that she couldn't wait any longer and that she had to tell me her big secret. She made me pinky swear not to tell anybody. (Technically, you're not anybody, so I'm telling you.)

Mary Ann said that she thinks Frank will pop the question soon and that if I didn't know what question she was talking about, it is the "Will you marry me?" question.

I knew there was something Joey wasn't telling me.

♡ *Mallory*

TUESDAY MORNING, AT MY DESK AT SCHOOL

Dear Diary,

On the way to school, I asked Joey if he knew of any questions that his dad was planning to ask Colleen.

Joey said his dad probably asks Colleen questions all the time because he always asks him questions like: Will you please do your homework? And will you please clean up your room?

I knew Joey didn't know I was talking about the will-you-marry-me question, so I asked Winnie.

When I asked her, she said she had a question to ask me.

Her question: Will you please leave me alone?

The whole way to school, I didn't ask one more question.

 Mallory

STILL AT MY DESK

Dear Diary,

Right now I'm supposed to be working on a list of all the words you can make out of the letters in Valentine's Day. Mrs. Daily said we're doing this since next Saturday is Valentine's Day and next

Friday, we're having our class Valentine's party. She says she wants us to start getting into the spirit of things.

But right now, I'm working on a different list. I'm working on a list of reasons why Frank should or should not "pop the question."

If Frank pops the question . . .

☐ YES:
1. Mary Ann and her mom will probably move here, and Mary Ann will be my next door neighbor, just like she used to be before I moved.

☑ NO:
1. Mary Ann and Joey will live in the same house.

2. Mary Ann and Joey will do everything together.

3. Mary Ann and Joey will do everything together . . . WITHOUT ME!

According to my list, it is not a good idea for Frank to pop the question.

 Mallory

<u>TUESDAY NIGHT, 7:14,</u>
<u>AT THE KITCHEN TABLE</u>

Dear Diary,

I'm supposed to be doing my homework. I'm trying to think about science, but the only thing I can think about is Frank popping the question, and I've decided something: I HAVE TO STOP HIM FROM DOING IT. I have to make sure if he does, there's only one thing Colleen

will say and that thing is, "NO WAY!"
 ♡ *Mallory*

TUESDAY NIGHT, 7:22, STILL AT THE KITCHEN TABLE

Dear Diary,

Now all I have to do is think of a way. How hard can it be?

 ♡ *Mallory*

WEDNESDAY NIGHT, 8:07, BACK AT THE KITCHEN TABLE

Dear Diary,

The answer is: VERY HARD. I've been trying since last night to think of a way to get Frank to NOT pop the question, and I can't think of a way. Not one, single way. Tonight, I ate spinach at dinner.

That's what Popeye does when he wants his muscles to work. I'm hoping it makes my brain work.

♡ *Mallory*

yuck!

THURSDAY NIGHT

Still no ideas. I'm never eating spinach again.

FRIDAY NIGHT

Dear Diary,

Still no ideas for how to stop Frank from popping the question.

I'm going to do what I always do when I have to do really hard thinking. I'm going to stop writing and start rubbing the sides of my head. That always helps me think.

♡ Mallory
FRIDAY NIGHT, 7:54,
STILL AT MY DESK

Dear Diary,

I've been rubbing my head for 14 minutes and I haven't thought of one single way to stop Frank from popping the question.

Got to go. Got to rub.

♡ Mallory.

me trying to think of a good idea

7:56
Still rubbing.

7:58
Still rubbing.

8:01
Still rubbing.

<u>8:07</u>

Dear Diary,

I've been rubbing my head for 27 minutes. I haven't gotten any ideas. The only thing I've gotten is a sore head. I'm going to pretend like I'm at the wish pond and make a wish. I wish I will think of a way in the next 5 minutes to stop Frank from asking Colleen to marry him.

I hope my wish will come true.

 Mallory

<u>8:11</u>

Dear Diary,

You won't believe what I'm about to tell you. MY WISH CAME TRUE! I thought of a brilliant plan to stop Frank from popping the question. I bet you can't wait to know what it is. So I'll tell you.

I'm going to write don't-get-married-to-each-other poems! One for Colleen and one for Frank. Once they read my poems, there's no way they'll want to marry each other. Don't you agree that my plan is brilliant?

Got to go. Got to write.

♡ *Mallory*

P.S. I'm going to sign my poems, Anonymous. (That means I'm not going to say who they're from.) YOU HAVE TO PINKY SWEAR NOT TO TELL ANYBODY!!!

Poems

FRIDAY NIGHT, 9:02, STILL AT MY DESK

Dear Diary,

It took a while, but I finally finished my don't-get-married-to-each-other poems. I wrote Colleen's on one piece of paper, and I put it in an envelope with her name on it. I did the same thing with Frank's poem. I'm going to mail them in the morning.

I think I did a really good job. Want to see what I wrote?

♡ Mallory

A poem for Colleen

Colleen, you do not want to marry poor Frank.
   He is so poor, he might rob a bank.
Colleen, you do not want to marry dumb Frank.
   He is so dumb, his mind is a blank.
Colleen, you do not want to marry bad Frank.
   He yells at his kids.
   They call him "The Crank."
Colleen, you do not want to marry cruel Frank.
   He does not keep water inside his fish tank.
Colleen, you do not want to marry "Your Frank."
   Take my advice and you'll have me to thank.

   If you marry him, you will be making a
Big, Big, **BIG** mistake!

   Sincerely,
   Anonymous

   P.S. I'm not making any of this up!

A poem for Frank

Frank, you do not want to marry Colleen.
   She dresses each day like it's Halloween.
Frank, you do not want to marry Colleen.
   When she blows her nose,
   her S-N-O-T is green.
Frank, you do not want to marry Colleen.
   There are rats in her kitchen.
   Her house is not clean.
Frank, you do not want to marry Colleen.
   She takes candy from babies.
   That lady is MEAN!
Frank, you do not want to marry "Your Colleen."
   If you marry that lady, you'll see what I
   mean.

   I'm just trying to save you from making
the BiggeSt mistake of your life.

Sincerely,
Anonymous

P.S. I'm not making
any of this up!

SATURDAY MORNING, AT MY DESK
SEARCHING EVERYWHERE!

Dear Diary,

My poems are gone! The envelopes
I left here last night with Frank and
Colleen's names on them are gone!

G.2.G. Got to go find my envelopes!

 Mallory

SATURDAY MORNING,
BACK AT MY DESK

Dear Diary,

The good news: I found my envelopes.

The bad news: I found one in Mom's
hands and the other one in Dad's.

When I went into the kitchen this
morning, Max was standing there with
a big grin on his face. "You're in HUGE
trouble," he said.

So I looked at Mom and Dad, who were

sitting at the kitchen table, to see if I could figure out what I did wrong, and that's when I saw that they had my envelopes, and they were OPENED! And you won't believe what they said.

mom: Dad and I are very upset that you would write these poems.

me: How do you know I wrote them? They're not signed by me. If you look at them, you will see that they are by ANONYMOUS!

max: They're in your handwriting. I found them in your room. And if you didn't write them, how would you know they are anonymous?

me: Shut up!

mom: Mallory, you're not allowed to say shut up.

max: So they <u>were</u> yours.

Dad: How do you think Frank and
    Colleen would feel if they read
    what you wrote?
me: I'm going to my room!
mom: Yes, you are, but not until you
    hear what we have to say first.

And then mom made me listen to a
whole long speech about how what I
wrote wasn't true and it was mean and
why you shouldn't do things like that and
how I needed to adjust my attitude and
lots more blah blah blah stuff about how
nice it is when two people fall in love.
THEN, she sent me to my room, which is
where I am now and will be for the rest
of the morning.
 Mallory

THE TALE OF THE GIRL WHO GETS INTO TROUBLE BUT DOESN'T DESERVE IT

Did you do this?

COLLEEN

I'm just a sweet child.

Go to your Room!

It's just you + me

Phone Calls

Dear Diary,

Mom finally let me out of my room because I had a phone call. Usually, I ♡ LOVE ♡ phone calls. But not this one. It was from Joey, and the reason I didn't like it was because of what he said.

Joey: Hey Mallory, does Mary Ann like to skateboard?

me: Why do you want to know?

Joey: You know she's coming here next weekend for the party, and Dad thought it might be fun to get a new skateboard for her if you think she'd like it.

What I said: Oh. (What I didn't say: I'd like a new skateboard too.)

Joey: You know how Dad likes doing nice things for people. He wanted to do something nice for Mary Ann.

me: (Even though it was my turn to say something, I didn't. I was too busy thinking about what Joey said about his dad doing nice things for people. It seemed to me that he likes doing nice things for one person, Mary Ann.)

Joey: Mal, you still there? Do you think you could call Mary Ann and find out? OK? I've got to go.

Then Joey hung up. Just like that. Before I even had time to say if I would or wouldn't call Mary Ann.

Since he didn't really give me a choice, I

dialed Mary Ann's number. S-L-O-W-L-Y.
When the phone started to ring, I waited
for Mary Ann to answer. But her mom
picked up.

Colleen: Mallory, how nice to hear
    your voice!
Me: May I speak to Mary Ann,
    please?
Colleen: Sweetie, she's in the car.
    We were just going out to do some
    shopping for next weekend. Mary
    Ann and I have a lot to do to get
    ready for the party.
What I said: Oh. (What I didn't say:
    I'm getting sick of people spending
    all their time getting ready for
    next weekend.)
Colleen: She'll call you when we get
    home, OK?

me: I just wanted to know if she wants to try skateboarding when she's here next weekend. But she probably doesn't. So don't even ask her, OK?

Colleen: No, I'm sure she'd love to. How nice of you to ask.

me: Actually, Frank is the one who asked. He wants to buy her a new skateboard.

Colleen: That Frank is sooooo sweet!

What I said: OK, bye. (What I wanted to say: Frank is really not sooooo sweet. If he asks you to marry him, you definitely should NOT!)

Then I hung up the phone and waited for Mary Ann to call me back. I waited for two whole hours.

While I was waiting, I got another phone call. This one was from Winnie.

me: Mary Ann?

Winnie: No, it's me, Winnie. Listen, I'm at the sporting goods store in the mall with Joey and Dad. They want to know if you talked to Mary Ann yet and if we should get her a skateboard.

me: No.

Winnie: No, what? No, you didn't talk to her? Or no, don't get her a skateboard?

me: Um, no, I haven't talked to her yet, so maybe you shouldn't get her a skateboard.

Winnie: Dad said if you haven't talked to her, we'll just get her the skateboard and something else too. Like a makeup kit. He said he's sure she'll like one of those things. He wants to get her something she'll

like. I can't think of one reason why
he should, but he says he's going to.

Then Winnie hung up and all I could do
was wait for Mary Ann to call me. And all I
could think about was the new skateboard
and makeup kit she was getting.

She didn't call until it was almost dinner
time, so I had a lot of time to think about
those things. And what I was thinking was
that it bothers me that the Winstons are
being so nice to Mary Ann and practically
ignoring me.

It's not like I don't want them to be nice
to her. But it's not like anybody is trying
to buy a new skateboard or a makeup kit
for me. It's kind of like they've forgotten
that I'm their next-door neighbor.

Just when I was thinking about how
they barely even know Mary Ann, and

how they're spending all of their time thinking of ways to be nice to her, mom told me to set the table (which isn't nearly as much fun as going shopping for a new dress or going to the mall to buy a new skateboard or makeup kit). I was putting down forks and knives when the phone rang. It was mary Ann (who was really in the mood to talk).

me: Hello.

mary Ann: Hey! Hey! Hey! Oh mallory, I'm so glad it's you. I have soooo much to tell you! First of all, mom and I just got home. We shopped all day. We both bought dresses for the party next weekend. Hers is purple and gold and it has a long skirt and a lacy top. mine is light pink on the top and dark pink on the bottom and it has a big bow on the back. We have so much to do to get ready for the party! On monday, we're going shoe shopping. On Tuesday, we're going present shopping for Joey and winnie and Frank. On wednesday, we're getting manicures. Real ones, at the salon. On Thursday, we're getting haircuts, and on Friday, I get to leave school at noon and we're driving straight to Fern Falls so I'll be there right when you get home from school. I can't wait till next weekend. I can't wait till we get to get all dressed up! we're going to have so much fun! It's going to be such a great party! And mom told me about the skateboard, and I can't wait to try skateboarding. It's

all so, so, so exciting! Don't you think
so too, Mallory? Don't you think
everything's going to be great, great,
great?

me: Um, yeah. Great, great, great.

Then I hung up the phone. Even
though Mary Ann is my best friend, this
seemed like one of those times when we
don't agree on everything.

♡ *Mallory*

MONDAY MORNING, STILL IN BED

Dear Diary,

I don't want to get out of bed today.

Actually, I don't want to get out of bed
for six more days.

Just six more days till Frank's party.

Just six more days till Colleen says three little letters, Y-E-S, that will change my life forever. Just six more days till my best friends become best step brother and sister, or whatever it is they become when their parents decide to get married.

I am staying in bed. Just six more days.

♡ *Mallory*

MONDAY, ON THE PLAYGROUND

Dear Diary,

This morning, Mrs. Daily reminded us that this Friday we're having our Valentine's class party since Saturday is Valentine's Day.

When she said that, Pamela leaned over to my side of the desk and said she can't wait because she loves Valentine's Day.

I know Pamela was waiting for me to say that I love Valentine's Day too. But I didn't. I used to love Valentine's Day. I don't anymore.

♡ *Mallory*

WHAT'S
SO GREAT
ABOUT
VALENTINE'S
DAY?

MONDAY,
AFTER SCHOOL AT MY DESK

Dear Diary,

On the way home from school, Joey asked if I wanted to do some skateboarding. "We can practice before Mary Ann gets here," he said.

I said, "Not today."

Then he asked if I wanted to take Cheeseburger on a walk with him and his dog, Murphy.

I said, "I don't feel like it."

So, he asked me if he could come over to my house. He said we could make super-sized peanut butter and marshmallow sandwiches.

But I said, "I'm not hungry."

Then Joey said, "Mallory, you love to skateboard and walk your cat and you're always hungry. You're not acting like yourself. Is everything OK?"

And then, I didn't say anything. I just shrugged my shoulders and nodded my head yes. But the real answer is no.

I just didn't feel like telling Joey that the reason I'm not acting like myself is because in exactly six days, his father is going to propose to Mary Ann's mother.

I can't even eat my favorite sandwich!

I didn't feel like telling him that if that weren't the case, I would be acting just like myself.

♡ *Mallory*

P.S. Today at school, mrs. Daily said that we need to make valentine's cards for everyone in our class to give out at the party. What am I going to write on Joey's card? I hope you have a SWEET year with my best friend as your new stepsister?

A Secret Admirer

TUESDAY AT SCHOOL,
IN THE SUPPLY CLOSET

Dear Diary,

You will never believe where I am.
I am hiding in Mrs. Daily's supply closet.

I had to come in here so NOBODY could see what I'm writing.

You won't believe what I am about to tell you.

I HAVE A SECRET ADMIRER! I know it's hard to believe but it's true. And the reason I know it's true is because my secret admirer gave me a secret card.

I found it when I came back from lunch. It was sitting right on top of my desk and it said "To Mallory From Your Secret Admirer" right on the envelope.

So I did the only thing I could do: I grabbed it off my desk and ran into the supply closet to read it.

I'm gluing it into my journal so NOBODY will ever be able to read it.

♡ Mallory

P.S. It worked out nicely that I'm in the supply closet. I hope mrs. Daily won't mind that I borrowed some of her glue.

Dearest Mallory,
I'm your secret admirer.
There's something I want to say.
I can't wait to celebrate
With you on Valentine's Day.
Hugs and Kisses!
Your Secret Admirer

OOPS

Dear Diary,

Sorry I ripped a page out of you when I tore out the card from my secret admirer, but I had to show it to Pamela.

I wasn't going to show it to anybody, but I showed her because I can NOT figure out who my secret admirer is and I wanted Pamela to help me.

Even though she makes better grades than I do, she couldn't figure it out either.

She said that if my secret admirer had written the card, we'd be able to look at the handwriting for clues. She said with the typing, it's kind of hard to tell.

I asked Pamela if she could check the fingerprints or something, but Pamela said she didn't know how.

I wonder who my secret admirer is.

 Mallory

P.S. I'm not showing anyone else my card. I will figure this out myself.

AFTER SCHOOL

Dear Diary,

I know I said I wasn't going to show anyone else the card from my secret admirer, but I showed Joey on the way home from school. I thought since he's a boy he might know if another boy in our class sent it.

But when I asked him, he started laughing. Then he said he didn't think another boy sent it. So I asked if he sent it.

He laughed even harder.

Then he said he didn't send it.

♡ *Mallory*

WEDNESDAY, BACK IN THE SUPPLY CLOSET

Dear Diary,

Guess what? It happened again! My secret admirer gave me something else. This time I got a little heart-shaped snow globe. I found it on my desk when I came back from lunch.

It snows pink snow and hearts when you shake it.

I LOVE it, except for one thing . . . I don't know who it's from!

I can't stand not knowing things!!! Especially things like who my secret admirer is. But I'm going to find out . . . AND SOON!

♡ Mallory

WEDNESDAY NIGHT

Dear Diary,

I tried finding out who my secret admirer is.

After math, I showed my snow globe to Mrs. Daily. I asked if she saw anyone leave this for me on my desk.

She said she hadn't, but that whoever did must like me a lot.

On the way home from school, I showed it to Joey. I asked if he was absolutely, positively, 100% certain that he's not my secret admirer.

He said he's absolutely, positively, 100% certain he's NOT my secret admirer.

After dinner, I showed it to max. Even though I didn't think he could possibly be my secret admirer, I just wanted to be sure.

I am sure.

♡ *Mallory*

THURSDAY AT SCHOOL,
IN THE BATHROOM

Dear Diary,

I still have not found out who my secret admirer is.

But there is something I did find. Another present. This time I got a little red plastic heart filled with Valentine's candy.

I found it sticking out of my backpack when we came back from recess.

♡ *Mallory*

P.S. I would have glued in the little red plastic heart filled with Valentine's candy, but it would have been hard to shut you, so I drew a picture instead.

P.P.S. I have to quit drawing pictures and start finding out who my secret admirer is.

THURSDAY NIGHT, AT THE DESK IN THE KITCHEN

Dear Diary,

I was sitting at the desk in the kitchen eating the candy (which was very delicious) from my secret admirer and making valentines for everyone in my class and feeling very happy (even though Max kept trying to eat my candy), when the phone rang.

It was Mary Ann, and right when I picked up I started to feel not so happy because she started telling me that she is so, so, so excited for this weekend and the party to get here. She asked me if I am so, so, so excited too. I said I was.

I wish I was.

I really wish I was.

I'm trying to be.

But I'm really not.

♡ *Mallory*

IN BED WITH CHEESEBURGER

Dear Diary,

I finished my valentines and got into bed. Ever since Mary Ann called, all I've been able to think about is this weekend. When you eat a big dinner, you go to bed with a full tummy. Tonight I'm going to bed with a full brain.

There are just so many questions in it right now. I feel like my brain is a parking lot and there are no empty spaces. I keep thinking:

What will it be like when Mary Ann is here this weekend?

Will she want to be with me or the Winstons?

What will happen if Frank proposes to Colleen?

Will that make them one big, happy family? And even though that's a lot of questions, I have one more.

Even though tomorrow is Valentine's Day, which is supposed to be happy, how can I act happy on the outside, when inside, I'm really not?

 Mallory

THE STORY OF THE GIRL WHOSE BRAIN WAS FULL!

ONCE UPON A TIME THERE WAS A GIRL.

SHE HAD A LOT OF QUESTIONS.

BUT NO ANSWERS.

POOR GIRL!

Valentine's Day

FRIDAY MORNING, STILL IN BED

Dear Diary,

Valentine's Day is almost here. When Mom and Dad came into my room to wake me up, they were all excited about this weekend. "Happy Day-Before-Valentine's Day!" said Mom.

But when I said that I didn't see what was so happy about it, Mom started listing all the things that she thinks I should be happy about.

"You have a party at school today. Mary Ann is coming into town tonight, tomorrow is Valentine's Day, and tomorrow night is the Winstons' party," she said.

When Mom said that, I didn't say anything back. The thing is, it's kind of hard for me to enjoy a party at school and my best friend coming into town and Valentine's Day and the Winstons' party, when all I can think about is Frank and how he's probably going to ask Mary Ann's mom to marry him, and that it's going to be a special Valentine's Day for a lot of people, but I feel like I'm not one of those people.

Then mom said that I have to be in the kitchen in ten minutes for a special Valentine's surprise.

I wonder if the surprise is that Frank's party has been cancelled.

 Mallory

AT THE KITCHEN TABLE

Dear Diary,
The surprise was heart-shaped

pancakes. Frank's party is still on.

G.2.G.2. school.

♡ *Mallory*

Love
and
Happiness

AT MY DESK

Dear Diary,

NEWSFLASH: On the way to school,
Joey asked me if I'm excited for mary
Ann to come into town. I said, "Of course,
she's my best friend."

Then, you won't believe what Joey said.

He said he's excited too, and that
when mary Ann gets here, he and mary

Ann and Winnie are writing a special song to sing at the party.

    NEW PROBLEM TO THINK ABOUT: If Mary Ann's mom and Joey's dad get married, will Mary Ann still be my best friend or will she be too busy doing things like writing songs with Joey and Winnie?

    Tra-la-la.

    ♡ *Mallory*

    P.S. Pamela just said that she can't wait until lunch is over and it's party time. Whoopee!

AT MY DESK, AFTER LUNCH

    Dear Diary,
    I just got back from lunch.

I was hoping this day would improve.

I was hoping my secret admirer would magically know that I'm not feeling so great and maybe leave me a secret surprise.

My secret admirer left one thing: NOTHING.

♡ *Mallory*

STILL AT MY DESK

Mrs. Daily just said that as soon as we finish math, we're going to start our party.

Pamela said she can't wait to finish math. Even though it's not my favorite subject, today I don't mind doing it. I'm more in a math mood than I am in a party mood.

♡ *Mallory*

I ♡ MATH

AT HOME, ON MY BED
WITH CHEESEBURGER

Dear Diary,

I just got home from school. I don't have much time to write because mom says Mary Ann and her mom should be here any minute.

I will quickly tell you about the Valentine's party at school. It will be easy to do quickly because there isn't much to tell. I wasn't in the mood for a party.

I wasn't in the mood to eat heart-shaped cookies with pink icing.

I wasn't in

the mood to eat chocolate candy with red sprinkles.

I wasn't even in the mood to read my Valentine's cards.

And I'm still not in the mood. My Valentine's cards are shoved into my backpack, which is where I put them during the party and where they will stay for good.

I will never be in the mood to read them.

I have to go. Mom is calling me. Guess who is here?

♡ *Mallory*

FRIDAY NIGHT, IN MY BATHROOM, NO TIME TO WRITE

Dear Diary,

This is going to be a quickie because Mary Ann is here and she doesn't even know I have you. I told her I was going to the bathroom while she gets ready for the fashion show. You heard right. She's going to model the dress she's wearing to the party tomorrow night.

 ♡ Mallory

FRIDAY NIGHT, IN BED WITH A FLASHLIGHT

Dear Diary,

I have to use a flashlight to write in you because Mary Ann is asleep next to me. She went to bed early because she said she wants to wake up early to go over to Joey's so they can work on the song. It's a good thing I don't have to get up early to work on a song because I CAN'T SLEEP!

♡ *Mallory*

P.S. I'm pretending like I'm at the wish pond and making a wish. I wish I will get bitten by bedbugs so I won't have to go to the party tomorrow night.

BED BUGS

A Party

Dear Diary,

I have three things to tell you.

One: I was not bitten by bedbugs.

Two: I'm still going to the party tonight.

Three: Mary Ann is at Joey's. Song writing.

♡ *Mallory*

8:47

Mary Ann is still at Joey's.

9:17

Still at Joey's. Still song writing.

9:56

MARY ANN IS STILL AT JOEY'S!

HOW LONG CAN IT TAKE TO WRITE A STUPID SONG?

10:18

Dear Diary,

Mary Ann is still at Joey's.

This is getting ridiculous. It is also rude. Mary Ann is a guest at my house and she is spending all of her time next door.

I'm going to call her and tell her to come home now.

I'm giving her three minutes, and then I'm calling.

♡ Mallory

10:21

It's been three minutes.

I'm going to give her three more minutes.

Then I'm definitely calling.

10:24

Three more minutes. That's it. Just three more minutes. I mean it.

10:27

One more three more minutes. Then that's really it.

10:31

Dear Diary,

It's been four minutes. I'm going to call now, but first I'm going to see if Mom or Dad or Max needs the phone. I don't want to be rude (like some people).

♡ *Mallory*

10:32

Dear Diary,

I just called. Joey answered the phone, so I asked him how the song for tonight was coming along. You won't believe what he said.

He said it wasn't! He said they tried to make up a song to sing at the party but they couldn't come up with anything so they ended up watching TV instead.

Can you believe that?!?!

I didn't even ask Joey the question I wanted to ask him, which was, "If you were just watching TV, why didn't you call me to come watch with you?"

I

didn't ask it because I already know the answer, which is: they're not even a family yet and they've already forgotten about me.

This is great. Just great.

♡ Mallory

SATURDAY AFTERNOON, IN THE PANTRY

Dear Diary,

I have exactly ten seconds to write in you. I have to go help Mary Ann get ready.

I have to help her zip her dress. I have to help her tie her bow. I have to help her put on her makeup.

Usually, I love helping Mary Ann. But tonight, I feel like Cinderella helping one of her stepsisters get ready for the ball.

💗 Cinder-Mallory

princess

SATURDAY NIGHT, IN MY CLOSET

Dear Diary,

I can't believe I found you.

It was hard because I had to look under the piles of clothes that Mary Ann left on the floor of my closet.

💗 Mallory

The tale of Cinder-Mallory

AT YOUR SERVICE

ZIP ME

MAKE ME UP

WHERE'S MY FAIRY GODMOTHER?

STILL IN MY CLOSET

Mom would have a meltdown if she saw this mess, but I'll have to clean it up later. It's almost party time.

Hopefully the party and the BIG secret won't be too bad. I have to quit writing now . . . so I can cross my fingers.

♡ *Mallory*

IN MY BED WITH CHEESEBURGER AND A FLASHLIGHT

Dear Diary,

It's 12:47 a.m. That's after midnight in case you haven't learned to tell time yet. It also happens to be the latest I've ever stayed up.

If Mom knew I was writing in you this late, I know she'd be even madder than if she saw the mess in my closet. But I can't sleep until I tell you about the party.

Mary Ann is sound asleep next to me.
And I'm really glad she is
because I have a lot to
tell you.

First of all, the party
was really red. Frank
put red roses all over
his house. There were
red roses in the living
room. There were
red roses in the dining
room. There were even red roses in
the bathroom!

The food was red too. Frank served
chicken with a red sauce and a salad with
miniature tomatoes. He had red drinks
too. Red wine for the grownups and
Shirley Temples for the kids. He even had
a big, red cake for dessert!

AND . . . Frank wore a red shirt. I know, it's hard to imagine him doing that, but he did!

There were TONS of people at the party. Everyone who lives on our street, some people that Frank works with, Joey's aunt and her kids, and of course, Mary Ann and her mom.

There was a band too. They played a lot of love songs that Frank said were just right for Valentine's Day. I don't think they were just right for any day, but a lot of the grownups looked like they liked that kind of music.

I could tell you more about the party, but I bet what you really want to hear is what the big secret was. So I'll tell you. Drum roll, please.

Joey's dad asked Mary Ann's mom to marry him!

You're probably not that surprised. And I wasn't either. I bet you want to know how it happened, so I'll tell you.

First, Frank banged his spoon on the side of his champagne glass. He had to bang for a long time till everyone was quiet. (I thought he was going to break his glass, but he got lucky.) Then, he told everyone he had an announcement to make.

That's when, in front of everyone, Frank got down on his knees and took Colleen's hand in his, and he said a bunch of lovey dovey stuff to her about how wonderful she is and how much he loves her, and then he said, "Colleen, will you marry me?"

And that made her start crying.

I thought she was crying because she didn't want to marry a guy who was losing his hair, and she felt a little funny telling him that after all the nice things he said about her.

But surprise, surprise. She started saying all kinds of nice stuff back about how special and kind he is and then she said, "Yes, my Frank, I will marry you." And she started crying even harder.

I asked mom why Colleen was being such a crybaby at a party. mom just hugged me and said they were happy tears. And when I looked at mom, she had some tears too, which she said were also the happy kind.

And when I looked around the room, they weren't the only people with happy tears in their eyes. Mr. Winston had some too.

Everybody looked happy. Joey looked happy. Grandpa Winston looked happy. Winnie, who almost never looks happy, looked sort of happy. And Mary Ann, who was jumping around and hugging everybody and screaming, "My mom's getting married!" looked particularly happy.

The only person who didn't look happy was Max, who said he can't believe he might have to live next door to Mary Ann (except he didn't call her Mary Ann, he called her Birdbrain, which is his favorite nickname for her) again. But when Frank brought out the big, red cake and said the party was just getting started, Max started smiling again.

While Frank and Colleen were passing around cake, everybody was talking and hugging and even though I felt kind of scared about what things would be like when the Winstons and Mary Ann and her mom become one family, I also felt a little happy. I don't exactly know why, except that everybody looked so happy, it just kind of made me happy too.

♡ *Mallory*

P.S. Even though I felt a little happy, I did not start crying. I didn't want to get tears in my cake.

P.P.S. I have 2 more things 2 tell you, but not anight. I am way 2 tired!!!!!!!!!!!!

A Heart-to-Heart

SUNDAY MORNING, AT THE WISH POND WITH CHEESEBURGER

Dear Diary,

I came out to the wish pond to write this because Mary Ann is still asleep and I didn't want to wake her up. Remember I told you that I had 2 more things to tell you?

Well, here's thing #1:

Last night, I had my first heart-to-heart.

Do you know what a heart-to-heart is? If you don't, don't feel too bad. I didn't either until last night when Joey said he wanted to have one.

It happened at the party while Frank and Colleen were passing out the cake. Joey asked me if I would take my piece to his room. He said he had something he wanted to talk to me about. So we went to his room and sat on his bed.

I started eating cake and Joey started talking.

First, he explained to me what a heart-to-heart is.

"A heart-to-heart is a talk you have with someone when they tell you what is going on in their heart and then you tell them what is going on in yours," he said. Then he told me he used to have these kinds of talks with his mom before she died.

I told Joey that that made me feel sad thinking about the talks he used to have with his mom, but he told me not to be too sad because the talk he wanted to have with me was a happy talk.

So I told him to go ahead and tell me what was on his mind.

"You haven't exactly been yourself since this whole thing with my dad and Colleen started," he said.

I put a big bite of cake in my mouth, so I wouldn't have to say why.

Joey kept talking. "Grandpa told me you might be feeling a little scared now that we're going to be a family, and that maybe you're worried you might be left out of things. Is he right?"

I didn't really want to tell Joey that that was exactly how I've been feeling, but since Grandpa Winston said it and everybody knows old people are usually right, I nodded my head yes, and I told Joey that that's exactly how I've been feeling.

Then Joey surprised me. He said he

had something he wanted to tell me and something he wanted to give me.

(I was hoping he would do the give-me part first, but he didn't.)

Here's what he told me: He told me that I wasn't the only one who is feeling scared. He said that he's feeling scared about some things too.

So I asked him what he's scared about,

and he told me. He said he's scared
thinking about what it will be like when
his dad and Mary Ann's mom get married
and they all live in the same house.

He said he's not sure he'll like sharing
his dad with Mary Ann and her mom.
He said he can't imagine what it will be
like having two more girls in his house. (I
told him that part sounded like fun, but
he said maybe not to him.)

Then, he said he's not sure what it will
be like having a mom because he hasn't
had one for a long time, and he doesn't
know if he will like having Colleen as his.

And then he said something that really
surprised me. He said that Winnie is
scared too.

I asked him how he knew that,
because one thing I knew for sure was
that Winnie didn't tell him. But Joey said

he knew because he heard Winnie talking to his grandpa, and he heard her say that she didn't want a new mother or a new sister, and that just thinking about what it will be like scares her.

And when he said that, it made me wonder. If Joey is scared and Winnie is scared, is Mary Ann scared too? Is she scared to move to Fern Falls? Does she feel afraid thinking about what it will be like to share her mom with Joey and Winnie? Is she nervous for Frank to be her dad?

Then I told Joey that I hadn't really thought about how all these changes would make anyone feel but me, but that I could see what he means about it all being scary for him too.

And then I told him if he ever wanted to talk about it with me, we could always have another heart-to-heart.

And that made Joey smile. Then he said he had something for me, but that first, he had a secret to tell me.

But I said, "No more secrets!"

So he said OK, and then he gave me something and guess what it was?

A giant chocolate Valentine's heart!!!!!!! (mmmmm!)

And it had a little card attached to it. I couldn't wait to eat the heart, but I knew I had to read the card first.

Wait till you see what it said!

BEST BUDS

Mallory—
I hope you
like the candy.
Happy Valentine's
Day!
—Your secret
Admirer

LOVE

believe it. "Joey, I don't get it. You said you weren't my secret admirer." I told him.

"I'm not," he said.

And that confused me. "Well if you're not, who is?" I asked.

And that question made Joey laugh.

"That's the secret I was trying to tell you," Joey said. "It's not just me. It's me and my dad and my sister and my grandpa. We're all your secret admirers."

I guess Joey could tell I was confused because he kept explaining.

"Do you remember the day we went to the mall to get the skateboard for Mary Ann? Well, Dad thought it would be nice to get something for you too. And it was my idea to do it as your secret admirer. We all thought you might like that."

I almost fell off Joey's bed when he said that. I mean, it's one thing to have a secret admirer. It's a whole other thing to have a secret admiring family. "Wow!" I said.

"We're not the in-love-with-you type of secret admirer," he said. "We're more the friendly-cheerer-upper type."

And that made a lot of sense to me. The Winstons were just trying to make me feel better about everything that's going on. So I thanked Joey and told him that he and his family are very good

WORLD'S BEST SECRET-ADMIRING FAMILY

friendly-cheerer-upper types of secret admirers. Then I told him that I was going to go thank the rest of his family.

But he said he had one more question to ask me before I left. He asked me if he could have a bite of my chocolate heart. But I told him he'd have to get his own chocolate heart. That this one was from my secret admirer!

♡ Mallory

Girl Talk

STILL AT THE WISH POND

Dear Diary,

Do you remember that I told you I had 2 things to tell you? Well, here's thing #2:

Last night, when Mary Ann and I got home from the party, I told her I wanted to have a girl talk.

She said she was way too tired for any kind of talk, but I told her I would do most of the talking and she could do most of the listening. So we put on our matching heart pajamas, got into bed, and I started talking.

I told her about the heart-to-heart that Joey and I had and how he said that he and Winnie are both kind of scared about what things will be like once his dad and her mom get married.

I told her I was really surprised when Joey told me that because ever since Frank and Colleen started being Frank and Colleen, I thought I was the only one who had any reason to be scared.

Then I told Mary Ann that now that I know that Joey and Winnie are scared, it makes me wonder if she's feeling scared too, and that since I'm her best, best, best friend, she can tell me if she is.

Even though Mary Ann said she was too tired to talk, she told me that what she's feeling is mixed. She said she feels scared about some things and happy about others.

Here's what she said
she's scared about:
1. Her mom being
   married to someone
   other than her dad.
2. Being part of a new family.
3. Having Winnie as a stepsister (she
   said she's really scared about that,
   and I don't blame her).

Here's what she said she's
happy about:
1. Seeing her mom so happy.
2. Having Joey as a
   stepbrother.
3. Moving to Fern Falls and
   living next door to her lifelong best
   friend. (She means me, in case you
   weren't sure.) She said that's what
   she's the very happiest about.

147

Mary Ann told me that she talked about a lot of this stuff with her mom, who told her that it's normal to feel mixed, because with most things in life, there are parts that make you feel happy and other parts that might not.

And when she said that, I told Mary Ann that mixed is how I feel too. I told her that even though the idea of her and Joey becoming part of the same family and living in the same house makes me feel kind of left out, the idea of her being my next-door neighbor again really makes me excited.

And when I said that, Mary Ann said something to me I hadn't thought of before. "Just think," said Mary Ann. "When I move in next door, we can have pajama parties just like the ones we used to have and just like the one we're having now, all of the time."

And when she said that, I didn't feel mixed at all. I just felt happy. "Sleep tight and don't let the bedbugs bite," I said to Mary Ann.

And she said it right back, like she always does when we have pajama parties.

Then I told Cheeseburger goodnight, and I turned out the light.

a new Poem

Dear Diary,

I wrote a new poem for Frank and Colleen. I hope they'll be happy when they see it, and I hope they'll be happy together. At first, I wasn't too thrilled about them being a couple, but the truth is, I think they make a pretty good pair.

I thought you might like a sneak peek at the poem.

♡ Mallory

Aren't they cute?

For Frank and Colleen

The Perfectest Pair

Frank and Colleen make THE perfectest pair!
Colleen loves Frank
   (though he's losing his hair).
Frank and Colleen make the perfectest pair!
Frank loves Colleen
   (like she's his teddy bear).
Frank and Colleen make the perfectest pair!
When they're not together,
   they're filled with despair.
Frank and Colleen make the perfectest pair!
Now that they're getting married,
   a life they will share.
Frank and Colleen make the perfectest pair!

   Big, huge hugs and kisses (I bet that's what
you're going to give each other now),
   ♡ Mallory

Party Pics

Dear Diary,

When I gave Frank the new poem I wrote about Colleen and him, Frank gave me something too. Some pictures from the party. Here's one of Mom and Dad and Max and me. I think we look pretty good when we're all dressed up (even Max).

Here's a picture of the Winstons and
mary Ann and her mom. I still can't
believe they're going to be one family now.

Frank even gave me pictures of me with Mary Ann and Joey. I guess there will be lots of pictures of the three of us together now that we're all going to be next-door neighbors.

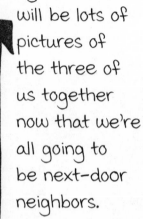

When he gave these to me, he said that even though sometimes things change, and soon Mary Ann and Joey will be brother and sister, some things never change, and Mary Ann and Joey will always be my friends.

But when he said that, I told Frank that he was wrong.

I told him that Mary Ann and Joey are not my friends, they are my BEST friends. My BEST, BEST, BEST friends.

And as far as I'm concerned, that will never, ever change.

♡ Mallory

Valentines

Dear Diary,

One more thing. Valentines! I finally got in the mood and opened mine. Boy, am I glad I did. I got cards from everyone in my class and trust me when I tell you, they're cute, cute, cute.

But don't take my word for it. See a few for yourself.

To Mallory,
We hope you have a *berry* happy Valentine's Day.
Love, Arielle and Danielle

TO THE WORLD'S BEST VALENTINE
-Joey

157

To a student who is all Heart.
Love, Mrs. Daily

See. Aren't they cute? I still do LOVE Valentine's Day and this one turned out to be great, even though I didn't think there was any way that it would.

There's something else I LOVE, and that is writing in you. I'm going to send

Grandma a great, big Valentine thank you card for giving you to me.

But guess what? I have to stop writing now. Mrs. Daily taught us the expression "That's all she wrote." She said it means that something is completely finished. And I am completely finished writing in you because I've used up all of the pages. No more room. BOO-HOO!

Thanks so, so, so much for being there when I needed you!

Big, huge hugs and kisses,
Mallory

P.S. I would love to end my journal with a P.S., but I can't actually think of one.
P.P.S. I still can't think of one.
P.P.P.S. I'm still thinking.
P.P.P.P.S. I still can't think of one, but it doesn't matter anyway because I'm officially out of room...

Darby Creek
A division of Lerner Publishing Group, Inc.
241 First Avenue North
Minneapolis, MN 55401 USA

For reading levels and more information, look up this title at www.lernerbooks.com.

Library of Congress Cataloging-in-Publication Data

Friedman, Laurie B.
    Heart to heart with Mallory / by Laurie Friedman ; illustrations by Barbara Pollak.
        p.   cm.
    Summary: Nine-year-old Mallory turns to her diary to sort through her emotions when she finds out she has a secret admirer and her two best friends' parents may be getting engaged.
    ISBN 978-1-57505-932-7 (lib. bdg. : alk. paper)
    ISBN 978-0-8225-7196-4 (EB pdf)
    [1. Best friends—Fiction. 2. Friendship—Fiction. 3. Remarriage—Fiction. 4. Valentine's Day—Fiction. 5. Diaries—Fiction.] I. Pollak, Barbara, ill. II. Title.
PZ7.F89773He 2006
[Fic]—dc22   2005034106

Manufactured in the United States of America
1-45461-39689-3/13/2018